WINNER OF THE TURNER
TOMORROW FELLOWSHIP

The narrator of this extraordinary tale is a man in search of truth. He answers an ad in a local newspaper from a teacher looking for serious pupils, only to find himself alone in an abandoned office with a full-grown gorilla who is nibbling delicately on a slender branch. "You are the teacher?" he asks incredulously. "I am the teacher," the gorilla replies.

Ishmael is a creature of immense wisdom and he has a story to tell, one that no human being has ever heard before. It is a story that extends backward and forward over the life span of the earth from the birth of time to a future there is still time to save. Like all great teachers, Ishmael refuses to make the lesson easy: he demands that the final illumination come from within ourselves. It begins with a simple but powerful question: Is it man's destiny to rule the world? Or is a higher destiny possible for him—one more wonderful than he has ever imagined?

On the following pages, readers respond to Ishmael . . .

"I felt like I met a friend when reading *Ishmael*."
—*Machelle Rogers, Friday Harbor, WA*

"I read *Ishmael* in 24 hours. With ecstasy and agony, sobs and cheers. To say thank you doesn't even come close."
—*Rachel Rosenthal, Los Angeles, CA*

"Whatever else is true in my life, I am very different since I read *Ishmael*."
—*Kathleen Sullivan, Hoffman Estates, IL*

"I am overwhelmed by your intelligent and inspirational book. I wish I had a child's version to read to my son, who is only three but absorbs everything."
—*Annabelle Stanley, Toronto, Canada*

"I have just finished *Ishmael* at one sitting and am overwhelmed by it. It demands closer reading and more careful contemplation."
—*James W. Watts, Mount Dora, FL*

ISHMAEL

Daniel Quinn

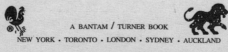

A BANTAM / TURNER BOOK
NEW YORK · TORONTO · LONDON · SYDNEY · AUCKLAND

ISHMAEL

A Bantam / Turner Book / June 1993

PUBLISHING HISTORY
Bantam hardcover edition published February 1992
Bantam paperback edition / August 1993

Maps by Eleanor Kostyk

Library of Congress Catalog Card Number 91-25441.

ISBN 0-553-56166-9

Published simultaneously in the United States and Canada

Bantam Books are published by Bantam Books, a division of Bantam
Doubleday Dell Publishing Group, Inc. Its trademark, consisting of the
words "Bantam Books" and the portrayal of a rooster, is Registered in
U.S. Patent and Trademark Office and in other countries. Marca Regis-
trada. Bantam Books, 1540 Broadway, New York, New York 10036.

PRINTED IN THE UNITED STATES OF AMERICA

OPM   0 9 8 7 6 5

FOR RENNIE

ONE

1

The first time I read the ad, I choked and cursed and spat and threw the paper to the floor. Since even this didn't seem to be quite enough, I snatched it up, marched into the kitchen, and shoved it into the trash. While I was there, I made myself a little breakfast and gave myself some time to cool down. I ate and thought about something else entirely. That's right. Then I dug the paper out of the trash and turned back to the Personals section, just to see if the damn thing was still there and just the way I remembered it. It was.

TEACHER seeks pupil. Must have an earnest desire
to save the world. Apply in person.

An earnest desire to save the world! Oh, I liked that. That was rich indeed. An earnest desire to save the world—yes, that was splendid. By noon, two hundred mooncalfs, soft-heads, boobies, ninnyhammers, noodleheads, gawkies, and assorted oafs and thickwits would doubtless be lined up at the address given, ready to turn over all their worldlies for the rare privilege of sitting at the feet of some guru preg-nant with the news that all will be well if everyone will just turn around and give his neighbor a big hug.

You will wonder: Why is this man so indignant? So bitter? It's a fair question. In fact, it's a question I was asking myself.

The answer goes back to a time, a couple decades ago, when I'd had the silly notion that the thing I most wanted to do in the world was . . . to find a teacher. That's right. I imagined I wanted a teacher—needed a teacher. To show me how one goes about doing something that might be called . . . saving the world.

Stupid, no? Childish. Naïve. Simple. Callow. Or just fundamentally dumb. In one so manifestly normal in other respects, it needs explaining.

It came about in this way.

During the children's revolt of the sixties and seventies, I was just old enough to understand what these kids had in mind—they meant to turn the world upside down—and just young enough to believe they might actually succeed. It's true. Every morning when I opened my eyes, I expected to see that the new era had begun, that the sky was a brighter blue and the grass a brighter green. I expected to hear laughter in the air and to see people dancing in the streets, and not just kids—everyone! I won't apologize for my naïveté; you only have to listen to the songs to know that I wasn't alone.

Then one day when I was in my mid-teens I woke up and realized that the new era was never going to begin. The revolt hadn't been put down, it had just dwindled away into a fashion statement. Can I have been the only person in the world who was disillusioned by this? Bewildered by this? It seemed so. Everyone else seemed to be able to pass it off with a cynical grin that said, "Well, what did you really expect? There's never been any more than this and never will be any more than this. Nobody's out to save the world, because nobody gives a damn about the world, that was just a bunch of goofy kids talking. Get a job, make some money, work till you're sixty, then move to Florida and die."

I couldn't shrug it away like this, and in my innocence I thought there had to be *someone* out there with an unknown wisdom who could dispel my disillusionment and bewilderment: a teacher.

Well, of course there wasn't.

I didn't want a guru or a kung fu master or a spiritual director. I didn't want to become a sorcerer or learn the zen of archery or meditate or align my chakras or uncover past incarnations. Arts and disciplines of that kind are fundamentally selfish; they're all designed to benefit the pupil—not the world. I was after something else entirely, but it wasn't in the Yellow Pages or anywhere else that I could discover.

In Hermann Hesse's *The Journey to the East*, we never find out what Leo's awesome wisdom consists of. This is because Hesse couldn't tell us what he himself didn't know. He was like me—he just yearned for there to be someone in the world like Leo, someone with a secret knowledge and a wisdom beyond his own. In fact, of course, there is no secret knowledge; no one knows anything that can't be found on a shelf in the public library. But I didn't know that then.

So I looked. Silly as it sounds now, I looked. By comparison, going after the Grail would have made more sense. I won't talk about it, it's too embarrassing. I looked until I wised up. I stopped making a fool of myself, but something died inside of me—something that I'd always sort of liked and admired. In its place grew a scar—a tough spot but also a sore spot.

And now, years after I'd given up the search, here was some charlatan advertising in the newspaper for the very same young dreamer that I'd been fifteen years ago.

But this still doesn't explain my outrage, does it?

Try this: You've been in love with someone for a decade—someone who barely knows you're alive. You've done everything, tried everything to make this person see that you're a valuable, estimable person, and that your love is worth something. Then one day you open up the paper and glance at the Personals column, and there you see that your loved one has placed an ad . . . seeking someone worthwhile to love and be loved by.

Oh, I know it's not exactly the same. Why should I have expected this unknown teacher to have contacted me instead of advertising for a pupil? Contrariwise, if this teacher was a charlatan, as I assumed, why would I have *wanted* him to contact me?

Let it go. I was being irrational. It happens, it's allowed.

2

I had to go down there, of course—had to satisfy myself that it was just another scam. You understand. Thirty seconds would do it, a single look, ten words out of his mouth. Then I'd know. Then I could go home and forget about it.

When I got there, I was surprised to find it was a very ordinary sort of office building, full of second-rate flacks, lawyers, dentists, travel agents, a chiropractor, and a private investigator or two. I'd expected something a little more atmospheric—a brownstone with paneled walls, high ceilings, and shuttered windows, perhaps. I was looking for Room 105, and I found it in the back, where a window would overlook the alley. The door was uninformative. I pushed it open and stepped into a large, empty room. This uncommon space had been created by knocking down interior partitions, the marks of which could still be seen on the bare hardwood floor.

That was my first impression: emptiness. The second was olfactory; the place reeked of the circus—no, not the circus, the menagerie: unmistakable but not unpleasant. I looked around. The room was not entirely empty. Against the wall at the left stood a small bookcase containing thirty or forty volumes, mainly on history, prehistory, and anthropology. A lone overstuffed chair stood in the middle, facing away, toward the wall at the right, and looking like something the movers had left behind. Doubtless this was reserved for the master; his pupils would kneel or crouch on mats arranged in a semicircle at his knee.

And where were these pupils, who I had predicted would be present by the hundreds? Had they perhaps come and been led away like the children of Hamelin? A film of dust lay undisturbed on the floor to disprove this fancy.

There was something odd about the room, but it took me another look round to figure out what it was. In the wall opposite the door stood two tall casement windows admitting a feeble light from the alley; the wall to the left, common with the office next door, was blank. The wall to the right was pierced by a very large plate-glass window, but this was plainly not a window to the outside world, for it admitted no light at all; it was a window into an adjacent room, even dimmer than the one I occupied. I wondered what object of piety was displayed there, safely beyond the touch of inquisitive hands. Was it some embalmed Yeti or

Bigfoot, made of cat fur and papier-mâché? Was it the body of a UFOnaut cut down by a National Guardsman before he could deliver his sublime message from the stars ("We are brothers. Be nice.")?

Because it was backed by darkness, the glass in this window was black—opaque, reflective. I made no attempt to see beyond it as I approached; I was the spectacle under observation. On arrival, I continued to gaze into my own eyes for a moment, then rolled the focus forward beyond the glass—and found myself looking into another pair of eyes.

I fell back, startled. Then, recognizing what I'd seen, I fell back again, now a little frightened.

The creature on the other side of the glass was a full-grown gorilla.

Full-grown says nothing, of course. He was terrifyingly enormous, a boulder, a sarsen of Stonehenge. His sheer mass was alarming in itself, even though he wasn't using it in any menacing way. On the contrary, he was half-sitting, half-reclining most placidly, nibbling delicately on a slender branch he carried in his left hand like a wand.

I did not know what to say. You will be able to judge how unnerved I was by this fact: that it seemed to me I should speak—excuse myself, explain my presence, justify my intrusion, beg the creature's pardon. I felt it was an affront to gaze into his eyes, but I was paralyzed, helpless. I could look at nothing else in the world but his face, more hideous than any other in the animal kingdom because of its similarity to our own, yet in its way more noble than any Greek ideal of perfection.

There was in fact no obstacle between us. The pane of glass would have parted like a tissue had he touched it. But he seemed to have no idea of touching it. He sat and gazed into my eyes and nibbled the end of his branch and waited. No, he wasn't waiting; he was merely *there*, had been there before I arrived and would be there when I'd left. I had the feeling I was of no more significance to him than a passing cloud is to a shepherd resting on a hillside.

As my fear began to ebb, consciousness of my situation returned. I said to myself that the teacher was plainly not on hand, that there was nothing to keep me there, that I should go home. But I didn't like to leave with the feeling that I'd accomplished nothing at all. I looked around, thinking I'd leave a note, if I could find something to write on (and with), but there was nothing. Nevertheless, this search, with the thought of written communication in mind, brought to my attention something I'd overlooked in the room that lay beyond the glass; it was a sign or poster hanging on the wall behind the gorilla. It read:

> WITH MAN GONE,
> WILL THERE
> BE HOPE
> FOR GORILLA?

This sign stopped me—or rather, this text stopped me. Words are my profession; I seized these and demanded that they explain themselves, that they cease to be ambiguous. Did they imply that hope for gorillas lay in the extinction of the human race or in its survival? It could be read either way.

It was, of course, a koan—meant to be inexplicable. It disgusted me for that reason, and for another reason: because it appeared that this magnificent creature beyond the glass was being held in captivity for no other reason than to serve as a sort of animate *illustration* for this koan.

You really ought to do something about this, I told myself angrily. Then I added: *It would be best if you sat down and were still.*

I listened to the echo of this strange admonishment as if it were a fragment of music I couldn't quite identify. I looked at the chair and wondered: *Would* it be best to sit down and be still? And if so, why? The answer came readily enough: *Because, if you are still, then you will be better able to hear.* Yes, I thought, that is undeniably so.

For no conscious reason, I lifted my eyes to those of my beastly companion in the next room. As everyone knows, eyes *speak*. A pair of strangers can effortlessly reveal their mutual interest and attraction in a single glance. *His* eyes spoke, and I understood. My legs turned to jelly, and I barely managed to reach the chair without collapsing.

"But how?" I said, not daring to speak the words aloud.

"What does it matter?" he replied as silently. "It's so, and nothing more needs to be said."

"But you—" I sputtered. "You are . . ."

I found that, having come to the word, and with no other word to put in its place, I could not speak it.

After a moment he nodded, as if in acknowledgment of my difficulty. "I am the teacher."

For a time, we gazed into each other's eyes, and my head felt as empty as a derelict barn.

Then he said: "Do you need time to collect yourself?"

"Yes!" I cried, speaking aloud for the first time.

He turned his massive head to one side to peer at me curiously. "Will it help you to listen to my story?"

"Indeed it will," I said. "But first—if you will—please tell me your name."

He stared at me for a while without replying and (as far as I could tell at that time) without expression. Then he proceeded as if I hadn't spoken at all.

"I was born somewhere in the forests of equatorial West Africa," he said. "I've never made any effort to find out exactly where, and see no reason to do so now. Do you happen to know the methods of Martin and Osa Johnson?"

I looked up, startled. "Martin and Osa Johnson? I've never even heard of them."

"They were famous animal collectors of the thirties. Their method with gorillas was this: On finding a band, they would shoot the females and pick up all the infants in sight."

"How terrible," I said, without thinking.

The creature replied with a shrug. "I have no actual memory of the event—though I have memories of still earlier times. In any case, the Johnsons sold me to a zoo in some small northeastern city—I can't say which, for I had no awareness of such things as yet. There I lived and grew for several years."

He paused and nibbled absentmindedly on his branch for a while, as if gathering his thoughts.

3

In such places (he went on at last), where animals are simply penned up, they are almost always more thoughtful than their cousins in the wild. This is because even the dimmest of them cannot help but sense that something is very wrong with this style of living. When I say that they are more thoughtful, I don't mean to imply that they acquire powers of ratiocination. But the tiger you see madly pacing its cage is nevertheless preoccupied with something that a human would certainly recognize as a thought. And this thought is a question: *Why?* "Why, why, why, why, why, why?" the tiger asks itself hour after hour, day after day, year after year, as it treads its endless path behind the bars of its cage. It cannot analyze the question or elaborate on it. If you were somehow able to ask the creature, "Why *what?*" it would be unable to answer you. Nevertheless this question burns like an unquenchable flame in its mind, inflicting a searing pain that does not diminish until the creature lapses into a final lethargy that zookeepers recognize as an irreversible rejection of life. And of course this questioning is something that no tiger does in its normal habitat.

Before long I too began to ask myself *why*. Being neurologically far in advance of the tiger, I was able to examine what I meant by the question, at least in a rudimentary way. I remembered a different sort of life, which was, for those who lived it, interesting and pleasant. By contrast, this life was agonizingly boring and never pleasant. Thus, in asking *why*, I was trying to puzzle out why life should be divided in this way, half of it interesting and pleasant and half of it boring and unpleasant. I had no concept of myself as a captive; it didn't occur to me that anyone was preventing me from having an interesting and pleasant life. When no answer to my question was forthcoming, I began to consider the differences between the two life-styles. The most fundamental difference was that in Africa I was a member of a family—of a sort of family that the people of your culture haven't known for thousands of years. If gorillas were capable of such an expression, they would tell you that their family is like a hand, of which they are the fingers. They are fully aware of being a family but are very little aware of being individuals. Here in the zoo there were other gorillas—but there was no family. Five severed fingers do not make a hand.

I considered the matter of our feeding. Human children dream of a land where the mountains are ice cream and the trees are gingerbread and the stones are bonbons. For a gorilla, Africa is just such a land. Wherever one turns, there is something wonderful to eat. One never thinks, "Oh, I'd better look for some food." Food is everywhere, and one picks it up almost absentmindedly, as one takes a breath of air. In fact, one does not think of feeding as a distinct activity at all. Rather, it's like a delicious music that plays in the background of all activities throughout the day. In fact, feeding became feeding for me only at the zoo, where twice daily great masses of tasteless fodder were pitched into our cages.

It was in puzzling out such small matters as these that my interior life began—quite unnoticed.

Although naturally I knew nothing of it, the Great Depression was taking its toll on all aspects of American life. Zoos everywhere were being forced to economize, reducing the number of animals to be maintained and thereby reducing expenses of all kinds. A great many animals were simply put down, I believe, for there was no market in the private sector for animals that were neither easy to keep nor very colorful or dramatic. The exceptions were, of course, the big cats and the primates.

To make a long story short, I was sold to the owner of a traveling menagerie with an empty wagon to fill. I was a large and impressive adolescent and doubtless represented a sensible long-term investment.

You might imagine that life in one cage is like life in any other cage, but this is not at all the case. Take the matter of human contact, for example. At the zoo, all the gorillas were aware of our human visitors. They were a curiosity for us, worth watching, in the way that birds or squirrels around a house might seem worth watching to a human family. It was clear that these strange creatures were there looking at us, but it never crossed our minds that they had come for that express purpose. At the menagerie, however, I quickly came to a true understanding of this phenomenon.

Indeed, my education in this regard began from the moment I was first put on display. A small group of visitors approached my wagon and after a moment began *speaking to me*. I was astounded. At the zoo, visitors had talked to *one another*—never to us. "Perhaps these people are confused," I said to myself. "Perhaps they've mistaken me for one of themselves." My wonderment and perplexity grew as, one after another, every group that visited my wagon behaved in the same way. I simply didn't know what to make of it.

That night, without thinking of it as such, I made my first real attempt to marshal my thoughts to solve a problem. Was it possible, I wondered, that changing my location had somehow changed *me*? I didn't feel in the least changed, and certainly nothing in my appearance seemed to have changed. Perhaps, I thought, the people who visited me that day belonged to a different species from those who had come to the zoo. This reasoning did not impress me; the two groups were identical in every way but this: that one group talked among themselves and the other talked to me. Even the sound of the talking was the same. It had to be something else.

The following night I attacked the problem again, reasoning in this way: If nothing has changed in me and nothing has changed in them, then *something else* must have changed. I am the same and they are the same, therefore something else is *not* the same. Looking at the matter this way, I could see only one answer: At the zoo there were many gorillas; here there was only one. I felt the force of this but could not imagine why visitors would behave one way in the presence of many gorillas and a different way in the presence of one gorilla.

The next day I tried to pay more attention to what my visitors were saying. I soon noticed that, although every speech was different, there was one sound that occurred over and over, and it seemed to be intended to attract my attention. Of course I was unable to hazard a guess as to its meaning; I possessed nothing that would serve as a Rosetta Stone.

The wagon to the right of mine was occupied by a female chimpanzee with an infant, and I had already observed that visitors spoke to her in the same way they spoke to me. Now I noticed that visitors employed a different recurrent sound to attract her attention. At her wagon, visitors called out, "Zsa-Zsa! Zsa-Zsa! Zsa-Zsa!" At my wagon, they called out, "Goliath! Goliath! Goliath!"

By small steps such as these, I soon understood that these sounds in some mysterious way attached directly to the two of us *as individuals*. You, who have had a name from birth and who probably think that even a pet dog is aware of having a name (which is untrue), cannot imagine what a revolution in perception the acquisition of a name produced in me. It would be no exaggeration to say that I was truly born in that moment—born as a person.

From the realization that I had a name to the realization that *everything* has a name was not a great leap. You might think a caged animal would have little opportunity to learn the language of its visitors, but this is not so. Menageries attract families, and I soon discovered that parents are incessantly schooling their children in the arts of language: "Look, Johnny, there's a duck! Can you say *duck*? D-u-u-c-k! Do you know what a duck says? A duck says *quack quack*!"

Within a couple of years I was able to follow most conversations within earshot, but I found that puzzlement kept pace with comprehension. I knew by now that I was a gorilla and that Zsa-Zsa was a chimpanzee. I also knew that all the inhabitants of the wagons were *animals*. But I could not quite make out the constitution of an animal; our human visitors clearly distinguished between themselves and animals, but I was unable to figure out why. If I understood what made us animals (and I thought I did), I couldn't understand what made them *not* animals.

The nature of our captivity was no longer a mystery, for I had heard it explained to hundreds of children. All the animals of the menagerie had originally lived in something called The Wild, which extended all over the world (whatever a "world" might be). We had been taken from The Wild and brought together in one place, because, for some strange reason, people found us interesting. We were kept in cages because we were "wild" and "dangerous"—terms that baffled me, because they evidently referred to qualities I epitomized in myself. I mean that when parents wanted to show their children a particularly wild and dangerous creature, they would point at me. It's true that they would also

point at the big cats, but since I'd never seen a big cat
outside a cage, this was not enlightening.

On the whole, life at the menagerie was an improvement
over life at the zoo, because it was not so oppressively
boring. It didn't occur to me to be resentful of my keepers.
Although they had a greater range of movement, they
seemed as much bound to the menagerie as the rest of us,
and I had no inkling that they lived an entirely different sort
of life on the outside. It would have been as plausible for
Boyle's law to have popped into my head as the notion that
I had been unjustly deprived of some inborn right, such as
the right to live as I pleased.

Perhaps three or four years passed. Then one rainy day,
when the lot was deserted, I received a peculiar visitor: a
lone man, who looked to be ancient and shriveled to me, but
who I later learned was only in his early forties. Even his
approach was distinctive. He stood at the entrance to the
menagerie, glanced methodically at each wagon in turn,
and then headed straight for mine. He paused at the rope
slung some five feet away, planted the tip of his walking
stick in the mud just ahead of his shoes, and peered intently
into my eyes. I have never been disconcerted by a human
gaze, so I placidly returned his stare. I sat and he stood for
several minutes without moving. I remember feeling an
unusual admiration for this man, so stoically enduring the
drizzle that was streaming down his face and soaking his
clothes.

At last he straightened up and gave me a nod, as if he'd
come to some carefully considered conclusion.

"You are *not* Goliath," he said.

At that, he turned and marched back the way he'd come,
without a look to right or left.

4

I was thunderstruck, as you may well imagine. *Not* Goliath? What could it possibly mean to be *not* Goliath?

It didn't occur to me to say, "Well, if I'm not Goliath, then who *am* I?" A human would ask this question, because he would know that, whatever his name, he is assuredly *someone*. I did not. On the contrary, it seemed to me that if I was not Goliath, then I must be no one at all.

Though this stranger had never laid eyes on me before that day, I didn't doubt for a moment that he spoke with an unquestionable authority. A thousand others had called me by the name of Goliath—even those who, like the workers at the menagerie, knew me well—but that was clearly not the point, counted for nothing. The stranger hadn't said, "Your *name* is not Goliath." He had said, "*You* are not Goliath." There was a world of difference. As I felt it (though I could not have expressed it this way at the time), my awareness of selfhood had been pronounced a delusion.

I drifted into a sort of fugue state, neither aware nor unconscious. An attendant came round with food, but I ignored him. Night fell, but I didn't sleep. The rain stopped and the sun rose without my noticing. Soon there were the usual crowds of visitors calling out, "Goliath! Goliath! Goliath!" but I paid no attention.

Several days passed in this way. Then one evening after the menagerie had closed for the day, I took a long drink from my bowl and soon fell asleep—a powerful sedative had been added to my water. At dawn I awoke in an unfamiliar cage. At first, because it was so large and so strangely shaped, I didn't even recognize it as a cage. In fact, it was circular, and open to the air on all sides; as I later understood, a gazebo had been modified to serve the purpose. Except for a large white house nearby, it stood alone in the midst of an attractive park that I imagined must extend to the ends of the earth.

It was not long before I'd conceived an explanation for this strange translocation: The people who visited the menagerie came, at least in part, with the expectation of seeing a gorilla named Goliath; how they came to have this expectation I could not guess, but they certainly seemed to have it; and when the owner of the menagerie learned that I was in fact *not* Goliath, he could scarcely go on exhibiting me as such, and so had no real choice but to send me away. I didn't know whether to be sorry about this or not; my new home was far more pleasant than anything I'd seen since leaving Africa, but without the daily stimulation of the crowds, it would soon become even more excruciatingly boring than the zoo, where at least I'd had the company of other gorillas. I was still pondering these matters when, around midmorning, I looked up and saw that I was not alone. A man was standing just beyond the bars, blackly silhouetted against the sunlit house in the distance. I approached cautiously and was astonished to recognize him.

As if reenacting our former encounter, we gazed into each other's eyes for several minutes, I sitting on the floor of my cage, he leaning on his walking stick. I saw that, dry and freshly dressed, he was not the elderly person I'd first taken him for. His face was long and dark and bony, his eyes burned with a strange intensity, and his mouth seemed set in an expression of bitter mirth. At last he nodded, exactly as before, and said:

"Yes, I was right. You are not Goliath. You are Ishmael."

Once again, as if everything that mattered was now finally settled, he turned and walked away.

And once again I was thunderstruck—but this time by a feeling of profound relief, for I had been redeemed from oblivion. More, the error that caused me to live as an unwitting impostor for so many years had been corrected at last. I had been made whole as a person—not again but for the very first time.

I was consumed with curiosity about my savior. I didn't think to associate him with my removal from the menagerie to this charming belvedere, for I was as yet incapable of even that most primitive of fallacies: *post hoc, ergo propter hoc.* He was to me a supernal being. To a mind ready for mythology, he was the beginning of what is meant by *god-like.* He had twice made a brief appearance in my life—and twice, with a single utterance, had transformed me. I tried to search for the underlying meaning of these appearances, but found only questions. Had this man come to the menagerie in search of Goliath or in search of me? Had he come because he *hoped* I was Goliath or because he suspected I was *not* Goliath? How had he so promptly found me in my new location? I had no measure of the extent of human information; if it was common knowledge that I could be found at the menagerie (as it had seemed to be), was it also common knowledge that I could now be found here? Despite all these unanswerable questions, the overwhelming fact remained that this uncanny creature had twice sought me out in order to address me in an unprecedented way—as a person. I was certain that, having finally settled the matter of my identity, he would vanish from my life forever; what more was there for him to do?

Doubtless you will have surmised that all these breathless apperceptions were just so much moonshine. Nonetheless the truth (as I later learned it) was not much less fantastic.

My benefactor was a wealthy Jewish merchant of this city, a man by the name of Walter Sokolow. On the day he discovered me at the menagerie, he'd been out walking in the rain, in a kind of suicidal gloom that had descended on him a few months before, when he learned beyond any doubt that his entire family had been swallowed up in the

Nazi holocaust. His wanderings led him to a carnival set up at the edge of town, and he went in with nothing in particular on his mind. Because of the rain, most of the booths and rides were shut down, giving the place an air of abandonment that accorded well with his melancholy. At last he came to the menagerie, whose chief attractions were advertised in a series of lurid paintings. One of these, more lurid than the rest, depicted the gorilla Goliath brandishing the broken body of an African native as if it were a weapon. Walter Sokolow, perhaps thinking that a gorilla named Goliath was an apt symbol for the Nazi giant that was then engaged in crushing the race of David, decided it would be satisfying to behold such a monster behind bars.

He went in, approached my wagon, and by gazing into my eyes, soon realized that I was no relation to the bloodthirsty monster in the painting—and indeed no relation to the Philistine tormentor of his race. He found it gave him no satisfaction whatever to see me behind bars. On the contrary, in a quixotic gesture of guilt and defiance, he decided to rescue me from my cage and fashion me into a dreadful substitute for the family he had failed to rescue from the cage of Europe. The owner of the menagerie was agreeable to a sale; he was even glad to let Mr. Sokolow hire away a handler who had looked after me since my arrival. The owner was a realist; with America's inevitable entrance into the war, traveling shows like his were either going to spend the duration in winter quarters or simply become extinct.

After letting me settle in for a day in my new surroundings, Mr. Sokolow returned to begin to make my acquaintance. He wanted the handler to show him how everything was done, from mixing my feed to cleaning my cage. He asked him if he thought I was dangerous. The handler said I was like a piece of heavy machinery—dangerous not by disposition but by dint of sheer size and power.

After an hour or so, Mr. Sokolow sent him away, and we gazed at each other in a long silence as we had already done twice before. Finally—reluctantly, as if surmounting some daunting interior barrier—he began to speak to me, not in the jocular way of visitors to the menagerie but rather as one speaks to the wind or to the waves crashing on a beach, uttering that which must be said but which must not be heard by anyone. As he poured out his sorrows and self-recriminations, he gradually forgot the need for caution. By the time an hour had passed, he was propped up against my cage with a hand wrapped around a bar. He was looking at the ground, lost in thought, and I used this opportunity to express my sympathy, reaching out and gently stroking the knuckles of his hand. He leaped back, startled and horrified, but a search of my eyes reassured him that my gesture was as innocent of menace as it seemed.

Alerted by this experience, he began to suspect that I possessed real intelligence, and a few simple tests were enough to convince him of this. Having proved that I understood his words, he leaped to the conclusion (as others were later to do in working with other primates) that I should be able to produce some of my own. In short, he decided to teach me to talk. I will pass over the painful and humiliating months that followed. Neither one of us understood that the difficulty was unsurmountable, owing to a lack of basic phonic equipment on my part. In the absence of that understanding, we both labored on under the impression that the knack would someday magically manifest itself in me if we persevered. But at last there came a day when I couldn't go on, and in my anguish at not being able to *tell* him this, I *thought* him this, with all the mental power I possessed. He was stunned—as was I when I saw that he'd heard my mental cry.

I won't burden you with all the steps of our progress once full communication was established between us, since they are easily imagined, I believe. Over the next decade, he taught me all he knew of the world and the universe and human history, and when my questions went beyond his knowledge, we studied side by side. And when my studies carried me beyond his own interests at last, he cheerfully became my research assistant, tracking down books and information in places that were of course beyond my reach.

With the new interest of my education to absorb his attention, my benefactor soon forgot to torment himself with remorse and so gradually recovered from his gloom. By the early sixties I was like a houseguest who needed very little attention from his host, so Mr. Sokolow began to allow himself to be rediscovered in social circles, with the not-unpredictable result that he soon found himself in the hands of a young woman of forty who saw no reason why he could not be made into a satisfactory sort of husband. In fact, he was not at all averse to marriage, but he made a terrible mistake in anticipation of it: He decided that our special relationship should be kept a secret from his wife. It was not an extraordinary decision for those times, and I was not sufficiently experienced in such matters to recognize it for the error it was.

I moved back into the gazebo as soon as it had been renovated to accommodate the civilized habits I'd acquired. From the first, however, Mrs. Sokolow viewed me as a peculiar and alarming pet and began agitating for my speedy removal or disposal. Luckily, my benefactor was used to having his own way and made it clear that no amount of pleading or coercion would change the situation he'd created for me.

A few months after the wedding, he dropped in to tell me that his wife, like Abraham's Sarah, was soon going to present him with a child of his old age.

"I anticipated nothing like this when I named you Ishmael," he told me. "But rest assured that I won't let her cast you out of my house the way Sarah cast your namesake out of Abraham's house." Nevertheless, it amused him to say that, if it was a boy, he would name him Isaac. As matters turned out, however, it was a girl, and they named her Rachel.

5

At that, Ishmael paused for so long, with his eyes closed, that I began to wonder if he'd fallen asleep. But at last he went on.

"Wisely or foolishly, my benefactor decided that I would be the girl's mentor, and (wisely or foolishly) I was delighted to have a chance to please him in this way. In her father's arms, Rachel spent nearly as much time with me as with her mother—which of course did nothing to improve my standing with that person. Because I was able to speak to her in a language more direct than speech, I could soothe and amuse her when others failed, and a bond gradually developed between us that might be likened to the one that exists between identical twins—except that I was brother, pet, tutor, and nurse all rolled into one.

"Mrs. Sokolow looked forward to the day when Rachel would begin school, for then new interests would make her a stranger to me. When this result didn't occur, she renewed her campaign to have me sent away, predicting that my presence would stunt the child's social growth. Her social growth remained unstunted, however, even though she skipped no fewer than three grades in elementary school and one grade in high school; she had a master's degree in biology before her twentieth birthday. Nonetheless, after so many years of being thwarted in a matter that pertained to the management of her own home, Mrs. Sokolow no longer needed any particular reason to wish me gone.

"On the death of my benefactor in 1985, Rachel herself became my protector. There was no question of my remaining in the gazebo. Using funds provided for this purpose in her father's will, Rachel moved me to a retreat that had been prepared in advance."

Once again Ishmael fell silent for several minutes. Then he went on: "In the years that followed, nothing worked out as it had been planned or hoped for. I found I was not content to 'retreat'; having spent a lifetime in retreat, I now wanted somehow to advance into the very center of your culture, and I proceeded to exhaust my new protector's patience by trying one bothersome arrangement after another to achieve this end. At the same time, Mrs. Sokolow was not content to leave things as they were and persuaded a court to cut in half the funds that had been allocated to my support for life.

"It was not until 1989 that things came clear at last. In that year I finally comprehended that my unfulfilled vocation was to teach—and finally devised a system that would enable me to exist in tolerable circumstances in this city."

He nodded to let me know this was the end of his story—or was as much as of it as he meant to tell.

6

There are times when having too much to say can be as dumbfounding as having too little. I could think of no way to respond adequately or gracefully to such a tale. Finally I asked a question that seemed no more or less inane than the dozens of others that occurred to me.

"And have you had many pupils?"

"I've had four, and failed with all four."

"Oh. Why did you fail?"

He closed his eyes to think for a moment. "I failed because I underestimated the difficulty of what I was trying to teach—and because I didn't understand the minds of my pupils well enough."

"I see," I said. "And what *do* you teach?"

Ishmael selected a fresh branch from a pile at his right, examined it briefly, then began to nibble at it, gazing languidly into my eyes. At last he said, "On the basis of my history, what subject would you say I was best qualified to teach?"

I blinked and told him I didn't know.

"Of course you do. My subject is: *captivity*."

"Captivity."

"That's correct."

I sat there for a minute, then I said, "I'm trying to figure out what this has to do with saving the world."

Ishmael thought for a moment. "Among the people of your culture, which want to destroy the world?"

"Which *want* to destroy it? As far as I know, no one specifically *wants* to destroy the world."

"And yet you do destroy it, each of you. Each of you contributes daily to the destruction of the world."

"Yes, that's so."

"Why don't you stop?"

I shrugged. "Frankly, we don't know how."

"You're captives of a civilizational system that more or less compels you to go on destroying the world in order to live."

"Yes, that's the way it seems."

"So. You are captives—and you have made a captive of the world itself. That's what's at stake, isn't it?—your captivity and the captivity of the world."

"Yes, that's so. I've just never thought of it that way."

"And you yourself are a captive in a personal way, are you not?"

"How so?"

Ishmael smiled, revealing a great mass of ivory-colored teeth. I hadn't known he could, until then.

I said: "I have an *impression* of being a captive, but I can't explain why I have this impression."

"A few years ago—you must have been a child at the time, so you may not remember it—many young people of

this country had the same impression. They made an ingen-
uous and disorganized effort to escape from captivity but
ultimately failed, because they were unable to find the bars
of the cage. If you can't discover what's keeping you in, the
will to get out soon becomes confused and ineffectual."

"Yes, that's the sense I have of it."

Ishmael nodded.

"But again, how does this relate to saving the world?"

"The world is not going to survive for very much longer as
humanity's captive. Does that need explication?"

"No. At least not to me."

"I think there are many among you who would be glad to
release the world from captivity."

"I agree."

"What prevents them from doing this?"

"I don't know."

"This is what prevents them: They're unable to find the
bars of the cage."

"Yes," I said. "I see." Then: "What do we do next?"

Ishmael smiled again. "Since I have told you a story that
explains how I come to be here, perhaps you will do the
same."

"What do you mean?"

"I mean, perhaps you will tell me a story that explains
how *you* come to be here."

"Ah," I said. "Give me a moment."

"You may have any number of moments," he replied
gravely.

7

"Once when I was in college," I told him at
last, "I wrote a paper for a philosophy class. I don't remember exactly what the assignment was—something to do with
epistemology. Here's what I said in the paper, roughly:
Guess what? The Nazis didn't lose the war after all. They

won it and flourished. They took over the world and wiped out every last Jew, every last Gypsy, black, East Indian, and American Indian. Then, when they were finished with that, they wiped out the Russians and the Poles and the Bohemians and the Moravians and the Bulgarians and the Serbians and the Croatians—all the Slavs. Then they started in on the Polynesians and the Koreans and the Chinese and the Japanese—all the peoples of Asia. This took a long, long time, but when it was all over, everyone in the world was one hundred percent Aryan, and they were all very, very happy.

"Naturally the textbooks used in the schools no longer mentioned any race but the Aryan or any language but German or any religion but Hitlerism or any political system but National Socialism. There would have been no point. After a few generations of that, no one could have put anything different into the textbooks even if they'd wanted to, because they didn't *know* anything different.

"But one day two young students were conversing at the University of New Heidelberg in Tokyo. Both were handsome in the usual Aryan way, but one of them looked vaguely worried and unhappy. That was Kurt. His friend said, 'What's wrong, Kurt? Why are you always moping around like this?' Kurt said, 'I'll tell you, Hans. There *is* something that's troubling me—and troubling me deeply.' His friend asked what it was. 'It's this,' Kurt said. 'I can't shake the crazy feeling that there is some small thing that we're being *lied* to about.'

"And that's how the paper ended."

Ishmael nodded thoughtfully. "And what did your teacher think of that?"

"He wanted to know if I had the same crazy feeling as Kurt. When I said I did, he wanted to know what I thought we were being lied to about. I said, 'How could I know? I'm no better off than Kurt.' Of course, he didn't think I was

being serious. He assumed it was just an exercise in epistemology."

"And do you still wonder if you've been lied to?"

"Yes, but not as desperately as I did then."

"Not as desperately? Why is that?"

"Because I've found out that, as a practical matter, it
doesn't make any difference. Whether we're being lied to or
not, we still have to get up and go to work and pay the bills
and all the rest."

"Unless, of course, you *all* began to suspect you were
being lied to—and *all* found out what the lie was."

"What do you mean?"

"If you alone found out what the lie was, then you're
probably right—it would make no great difference. But if
you *all* found out what the lie was, it might conceivably
make a very great difference indeed."

"True."

"Then that is what we must hope for."

I started to ask him what he meant by that, but he held up
a leathery black hand and told me: "Tomorrow."

8

That evening I went for a walk. To walk for
the sake of walking is something I seldom do. Inside my
apartment I'd felt inexplicably anxious. I needed to talk to
someone, to be reassured. Or perhaps I needed to confess
my sin: I was once again having impure thoughts about
saving the world. Or it was neither of these—I was afraid I
was dreaming. Indeed, considering the events of the day, it
was likely that I was dreaming. I sometimes fly in my
dreams, and each time I say to myself, "At last—it's happening *in reality* and not in a dream!"

In any case, I needed to talk to someone, and I was alone.
This is my habitual condition, by choice—or so I tell myself.

Mere acquaintanceship leaves me unsatisfied, and few people are willing to accept the burdens and risks of friendship as I conceive of it.

People say that I'm sour and misanthropic, and I tell them they're probably right. Argument of any sort, on any subject, has always seemed like a waste of time to me.

The next morning I woke and thought: "Even so, it *could* be a dream. One can sleep in a dream, even have dreams in a dream." As I went through the motions of making breakfast, eating, and washing up, my heart was pounding furiously. It seemed to be saying, "How can you pretend not to be terrified?"

The time passed. I drove downtown. The building was still there. The office at the end of the hall on the ground floor was still there and still unlocked.

When I opened the door, Ishmael's huge, meaty aroma came down on me like a thunderclap. On wobbly legs, I walked to the chair and sat down.

Ishmael studied me gravely through the dark glass, as if wondering if I was strong enough to be taxed with serious conversation. When he made up his mind, he began without preamble of any kind, and I came to know that this was his usual style.

TWO

1

"Oddly enough," he said, "it was my bene-
factor who awakened my interest in the subject of captivity
and not my own condition. As I may have indicated in
yesterday's narrative, he was obsessed by the events then
taking place in Nazi Germany."

"Yes, that's what I gathered."

"From your story about Kurt and Hans yesterday, I take
it that you're a student of the life and times of the German
people under Adolf Hitler."

"A student? No, I wouldn't go as far as that. I've read some of the well-known books—Speer's memoirs, *Rise and Fall of the Third Reich*, and so on—and a few studies of Hitler."

"In that case, I'm sure you understand what Mr. Sokolow was at pains to show me: that it was not only the Jews who were captives under Hitler. The entire German nation was a captive, including his enthusiastic supporters. Some detested what he was doing, some just shambled on as best they could, and some positively thrived on it—but they were all his captives."

"I think I see what you mean."

"What was it that held them captive?"

"Well . . . terror, I suppose."

Ishmael shook his head. "You must have seen films of the prewar rallies, with hundreds of thousands of them singing and cheering as one. It wasn't terror that brought them to those feasts of unity and power."

"True. Then I'd have to say it was Hitler's charisma."

"He certainly had that. But charisma only wins people's attention. Once you have their attention, you have to have something to tell them. And what did Hitler have to tell the German people?"

I pondered this for a few moments without any real conviction. "Apart from the Jewish business, I don't think I could answer that question."

"What he had to tell them was a story."

"A story."

"A story in which the Aryan race and the people of Germany in particular had been deprived of their rightful place in the world, bound, spat upon, raped, and ground into the dirt under the heels of mongrel races, Communists, and Jews. A story in which, under the leadership of Adolf Hitler, the Aryan race would burst its bonds, wreak vengeance on its oppressors, purify mankind of its defilements, and assume its rightful place as the master of all races."

"True."

"It may seem incredible to you now that any people could have been captivated by such nonsense, but after nearly two decades of degradation and suffering following World War I, it had an almost overwhelming appeal to the people of Germany, and it was reinforced not only through the ordinary means of propaganda but by an intensive program of education of the young and reeducation of the old."

"True."

"As I say, there were many in Germany who recognized this story as rank mythology. They were nevertheless held captive by it simply because the vast majority around them thought it sounded wonderful and were willing to give their lives to make it a reality. Do you see what I mean?"

"I think so. Even if you weren't personally captivated by the story, you were a captive all the same, because the people around you *made* you a captive. You were like an animal being swept along in the middle of a stampede."

"That's right. Even if you privately thought the whole thing was madness, you had to play your part, you had to take your place in the story. The only way to avoid that was to escape from Germany entirely."

"True."

"Do you understand why I'm telling you this?"

"I think so, but I'm not sure."

"I'm telling you this because the people of your culture are in much the same situation. Like the people of Nazi Germany, they are the captives of a story."

I sat there blinking for a while. "I know of no such story," I told him at last.

"You mean you've never heard of it?"

"That's right."

Ishmael nodded. "That's because there's no *need* to hear of it. There's no need to name it or discuss it. Every one of you knows it by heart by the time you're six or seven. Black and white, male and female, rich and poor, Christian and

Jew, American and Russian, Norwegian and Chinese, you all hear it. And you hear it incessantly, because every medium of propaganda, every medium of education pours it out incessantly. And hearing it incessantly, you don't listen to it. There's no *need* to listen to it. It's always there humming away in the background, so there's no need to attend to it at all. In fact, you'll find—at least initially—that it's *hard* to attend to it. It's like the humming of a distant motor that never stops; it becomes a sound that's no longer heard at all."

"This is very interesting," I told him. "But it's also a little hard to believe."

Ishmael's eyes closed gently in an indulgent smile. "Belief is not required. Once you know this story, you'll hear it everywhere in your culture, and you'll be astonished that the people around you don't hear it as well but merely take it in."

2

"Yesterday you told me you have the *impression* of being a captive. You have this impression because there is enormous pressure on you to take a place in the story your culture is enacting in the world—any place at all. This pressure is exerted in all sorts of ways, on all sorts of levels, but it's exerted most basically this way: Those who refuse to take a place do not get fed."

"Yes, that's so."

"A German who couldn't bring himself to take a place in Hitler's story had an option: He could leave Germany. You don't have that option. Anywhere you go in the world, you'll find the same story being enacted, and if you don't take a place in it you won't get fed."

"True."

"Mother Culture teaches you that this is as it should be.

Except for a few thousand savages scattered here and there, all the peoples of the earth are now enacting this story. This is the story man was born to enact, and to depart from it is to resign from the human race itself, is to venture into oblivion. Your place is *here,* participating in this story, putting your shoulder to the wheel, and as a reward, being fed. There is no 'something else.' To step out of this story is to fall off the edge of the world. There's no way out of it except through death."

"Yes, that's the way it seems."

Ishmael paused to think for a bit. "All this is just a preface to our work. I wanted you to hear it because I wanted you to have at least a vague idea of what you're getting into here. Once you learn to discern the voice of Mother Culture humming in the background, telling her story over and over again to the people of your culture, you'll never stop being conscious of it. Wherever you go for the rest of your life, you'll be tempted to say to the people around you, 'How can you listen to this stuff and not recognize it for what it is?' And if you do this, people will look at you oddly and wonder what the devil you're talking about. In other words, if you take this educational journey with me, you're going to find yourself alienated from the people around you—friends, family, past associates, and so on."

"That I can stand," I told him, and let it go at that.

3

"It is my most heartfelt and unattainable fantasy to travel once in your world as you do, freely and unobtrusively—to step out onto a street and flag down a taxi to take me to the airport, where I would board a flight to New York or London or Florence. Much of this fantasy is spent in making delicious preparations for the journey, in pondering what must accompany me in my luggage and what may be safely left behind. (You understand that I would of course be traveling in human disguise.) If I take too much, dragging it from place to place will be tiresome; on the other hand, if I take too little, I will forever be having to break my journey to pick up things along the way—and that will be even more tiresome."

"True," I said, just to be agreeable.

"That's what today is for: We're packing a bag for our journey together. I'm going to throw into this bag some things I won't want to stop and pick up later on. These things will mean little or nothing to you right now. I'll just show them to you briefly and then toss them into the bag. That way you'll recognize them when I take them out later on."

"Okay."

"First, some vocabulary. Let's have some names so we don't have to go on talking about 'the people of your culture' and 'the people of all other cultures.' I've used various names with various pupils, but I'm going to try a new pair with you. You're familiar with the expression 'Take it or leave it.' Using them in this sense, do the words *takers* and *leavers* have any heavy connotation for you?"

"I'm not sure what you mean."

"I mean, if I call one group Takers and the other group Leavers, will this sound like I'm setting up one to be good guys and the other to be bad guys?"

"No. They sound pretty neutral to me."

"Good. So henceforth I'm going to call the people of your culture Takers and the people of all other cultures Leavers."

I hmm'ed a bit. "I have a problem with that."

"Speak."

"I don't see how you can lump everyone else in the world into one category like that."

"This is the way it's done in your own culture, except that you use a pair of heavily loaded terms instead of these

relatively neutral terms. You call yourselves *civilized* and all
the rest *primitive*. You are universally agreed on these
terms; I mean that the people of London and Paris and
Baghdad and Seoul and Detroit and Buenos Aires and
Toronto all know that—whatever else separates them—
they are united in being *civilized* and distinct from Stone
Age peoples scattered all over the world; you consider or
recognize that, whatever their differences, these Stone Age
peoples are likewise united in being *primitive*."

"Yes, that's right."

"Would you be more comfortable if we used these terms,
civilized and *primitive*?"

"Yes, I suppose I would be, but only because I'm used to
them. Takers and Leavers is fine with me."

4

"Second: the map. I have it. You don't have
to memorize the route. In other words, don't worry if, at the
end of any day, you suddenly realize that you can't remember a word I've said. That doesn't matter. It's the journey
itself that's going to change you. Do you see what I mean?"

"I'm not sure."

Ishmael thought for a moment. "I'll give you a general
idea of where we're heading, then you'll understand."

"Okay."

"Mother Culture, whose voice has been in your ear since
the day of your birth, has given you an explanation of *how
things came to be this way*. You know it well; everyone in
your culture knows it well. But this explanation wasn't given
to you all at once. No one ever sat you down and said, 'Here
is how things came to be this way, beginning ten or fifteen
billion years ago right up to the present.' Rather, you assembled this explanation like a mosaic: from a million bits of
information presented to you in various ways by others who

share that explanation. You assembled it from the table talk
of your parents, from cartoons you watched on television,
from Sunday School lessons, from your textbooks and
teachers, from news broadcasts, from movies, novels, ser-
mons, plays, newspapers, and all the rest. Are you with me
so far?"

"I think so."

"This explanation of *how things came to be this way* is
ambient in your culture. Everyone knows it and everyone
accepts it without question."

"Okay."

"As we make our journey here, we're going to be reex-
amining key pieces of that mosaic. We're going to be taking
them out of your mosaic and fitting them into an entirely
different mosaic: into an entirely different explanation of
how things came to be this way."

"Okay."

"And when we're finished, you'll have an entirely new
perception of the world and of all that's happened here.
And it won't matter in the least whether you remember how
that perception was assembled. The journey itself is going
to change you, so you don't have to worry about memorizing
the route we took to accomplish that change."

"Right. I see what you mean now."

5

"Third," he said, "definitions. These are
words that will have a special meaning in our discourse
here. First definition: *story*. A story is a scenario interrelating man, the world, and the gods."

"Okay."

"Second definition: *to enact*. To enact a story is to live so
as to make the story a reality. In other words, to enact a story
is to strive to make it come true. You recognize that this is

what the people of Germany were doing under Hitler. They were trying to make the Thousand Year Reich a reality. They were trying to make the story he was telling them come true."

"Right."

"Third definition: *culture*. A culture is a people enacting a story."

"A people enacting a story. And a story again is . . . ?"

"A scenario interrelating man, the world, and the gods."

"Okay. So you're saying that the people of my culture are enacting their own story about man, the world, and the gods."

"That's right."

"But I still don't know what that story is."

"You will. Don't fret about it. For the moment all you have to know is that two fundamentally different stories have been enacted here during the lifetime of man. One began to be enacted here some two or three million years ago by the people we've agreed to call Leavers and is still being enacted by them today, as successfully as ever. The other began to be enacted here some ten or twelve thousand years ago by the people we've agreed to call Takers, and is apparently about to end in catastrophe."

"Ah," I said, meaning I know not what.

6

"If Mother Culture were to give an account of human history using these terms, it would go something like this: 'The Leavers were chapter one of human history—a long and uneventful chapter. Their chapter of human history ended about ten thousand years ago with the birth of agriculture in the Near East. This event marked the beginning of chapter two, the chapter of the Takers. It's true there are still Leavers living in the world, but these are anachronisms, fossils—people living in the past, people who just don't realize that their chapter of human history is over.'"

"Right."

"This is the general shape of human history as it's perceived in your culture."

"I would say so."

"As you'll come to see, what I'm saying is quite different from this. The Leavers are not chapter one of a story in which the Takers are chapter two."

"Say that again?"

"I'll say it differently. The Leavers and the Takers are enacting two separate stories, based on entirely different and contradictory premises. This is something we'll be looking at later, so you don't have to understand it right this second."

"Okay."

7

Ishmael scratched the side of his jaw thoughtfully. From my side of the glass, I heard nothing of this; in imagination it sounded like a shovel being dragged across gravel.

"I think our bag is packed. As I said, I don't expect you to remember everything I've thrown into it today. When you leave here, everything will probably all just turn into one great muddle."

"I believe you," I said with conviction.

"But that's all right. If I pull something from our bag tomorrow that I put in today, you'll recognize it instantly, and that's all that matters."

"Okay. I'm glad to hear it."

"We'll make this a short session today. The journey itself begins tomorrow. Meanwhile, you can spend the rest of today groping for the story the people of your culture have been enacting in the world for the past ten thousand years. Do you remember what it's about?"

"About?"

"It's about the meaning of the world, about divine intentions in the world, and about human destiny."

"Well, I can tell you *stories* about these things, but I don't know any *one* story."

"It's the one story that everyone in your culture knows and accepts."

"I'm afraid that doesn't help much."

"Perhaps it'll help if I tell you that it's an *explaining* story, like 'How the Elephant Got Its Trunk' or 'How the Leopard Got Its Spots.'"

"Okay."

"And what do you suppose this story of yours explains?"

"God, I have no idea."

"That should be clear from what I've already told you. It explains *how things came to be this way*. From the beginning until now."

"I see," I said, and stared out the window for a while. "I'm certainly not aware of knowing such a story. As I said, *stories,* yes, but nothing like a *single* story."

Ishmael pondered this for a minute or two. "One of the pupils I mentioned yesterday felt obliged to explain to me what she was looking for, and she said, 'Why is it that no one is excited? I hear people talking in the Laundromat about the end of the world, and they're no more excited than if they were comparing detergents. People talk about the destruction of the ozone layer and the death of all life. They talk about the devastation of the rain forests, about deadly pollution that will be with us for thousands and millions of years, about the disappearance of dozens of species of life every day, about the end of speciation itself. And they seem perfectly calm.'

"I said to her, 'Is this what you want to know then—why

people aren't excited about the destruction of the world?' She thought about that for a while and said, 'No, I know why they're not excited. They're not excited because they believe what they've been told.'"

I said, "Yes?"

"What have people been told that keeps them from becoming excited, that keeps them relatively calm when they view the catastrophic damage they're inflicting on this planet?"

"I don't know."

"They've been told an explaining story. They've been given an explanation of *how things came to be this way,* and this stills their alarm. This explanation covers everything, including the deterioration of the ozone layer, the pollution of the oceans, the destruction of the rain forests, and even human extinction—and it satisfies them. Or perhaps it would be more accurate to say that it *pacifies* them. They put their shoulders to the wheel during the day, stupefy themselves with drugs or television at night, and try not to think too searchingly about the world they're leaving their children to cope with."

"Right."

"You yourself were given the same explanation of *how things came to be this way* as everyone else—but it apparently doesn't satisfy you. You've heard it from infancy but have never managed to swallow it. You have the feeling something's been left out, glossed over. You have the feeling you've been lied to about something, and if you can, you'd like to know what it is—and that's what you're doing here in this room."

"Let me think about this for a second. Are you saying that this explaining story contains the lies I was talking about in my paper about Kurt and Hans?"

"That's right. That's it exactly."

"This boggles my mind. I don't know any such story. Not any *single* story."

"It's a single, perfectly unified story. You just have to think mythologically."

"What?"

"I'm talking about your culture's mythology, of course. I thought that was obvious."

"It wasn't obvious to me."

"Any story that explains the meaning of the world, the intentions of the gods, and the destiny of man is bound to be mythology."

"That may be so, but I'm not aware of anything remotely like that. As far as I know, there's nothing in our culture that could be called mythology, unless you're talking about Greek mythology or Norse mythology or something like that."

"I'm talking about *living* mythology. Not recorded in any book—recorded in the minds of the people of your culture, and being enacted all over the world even as we sit here and speak of it."

"Again, as far as I know, there's nothing like that in our culture."

Ishmael's tarry forehead crinkled into furrows as he gave me a look of amused exasperation. "This is because you think of mythology as a set of fanciful tales. The Greeks didn't think of their mythology this way. Surely you must realize that. If you went up to a man of Homeric Greece and asked him what fanciful tales he told his children about the gods and the heroes of the past, he wouldn't know what you were talking about. He'd say what you said: 'As far as I know, there's nothing like that in our culture.' A Norseman would have said the same."

"Okay. But that doesn't exactly help."

"All right. Let's cut the assignment down to a more modest size. This story, like every story, has a beginning, a middle, and an end. And each of these parts is a story in itself. Before we get together tomorrow, see if you can find the beginning of the story."

"The beginning of the story."

"Yes. Think . . . anthropologically."

I laughed. "What does that mean?"

"If you were an anthropologist after the story being enacted by the Alawa aborigines of Australia, you would expect to hear a story with a beginning, a middle, and an end."

"Okay."

"And what would you expect the beginning of the story to be?"

"I have no idea."

"Of course you do. You're just playing dumb."

I sat there for a minute, trying to figure out how to stop playing dumb. "Okay," I said at last. "I guess I'd expect it to be their creation myth."

"Of course."

"But I don't see how that helps me."

"Then I'll spell it out. You're looking for your own culture's creation myth."

I stared at him balefully. "We *have* no creation myth," I said. "That's a certainty."

THREE

1

"What's that?" I said when I arrived the following morning. I was referring to an object resting on the arm of my chair.

"What does it look like?"

"A tape recorder."

"That's exactly what it is."

"I mean, what's it for?"

"It's for recording for posterity the curious folktales of a doomed culture, which you are going to tell me."

I laughed and sat down. "I'm afraid I haven't as yet found any curious folktales to tell you."

"My suggestion that you look for a creation myth bore no fruit?"

"We have no creation myth," I said again. "Unless you're talking about the one in Genesis."

"Don't be absurd. If an eighth-grade teacher invited you to explain how all this began, would you read the class the first chapter of Genesis?"

"Certainly not."

"Then what account *would* you give them?"

"I could give them an account, but it certainly wouldn't be a *myth*."

"Naturally you wouldn't consider it a myth. No creation story is a myth to the people who tell it. It's just *the story*."

"Okay, but the story I'm talking about is definitely not a myth. Parts of it are still in question, I suppose, and I suppose later research might make some revisions in it, but it's certainly not a myth."

"Turn on the tape recorder and begin. Then we'll know."

I gave him a reproachful look. "You mean you actually want me to . . . uh . . ."

"To tell the story, that's right."

"I can't just reel it off. I need some time to get it to-gether."

"There's plenty of time. It's a ninety-minute tape."

I sighed, turned on the recorder, and closed my eyes.

2

"It all started a long time ago, ten or fifteen billion years ago," I began a few minutes later. "I'm not current on which theory is in the lead, the steady-state or the big-bang, but in either case the universe began a long time ago."

At that point I opened my eyes and gave Ishmael a speculative look.

He gave me one back and said, "Is that it? Is that the story?"

"No, I was just checking." I closed my eyes and began again. "And then, I don't know—I guess about six or seven billion years ago—our own solar system was born. . . . I have a picture in my mind from some childhood encyclopedia of blobs being thrown out or blobs coalescing . . . and these were the planets. Which, over the next couple billion years, cooled and solidified. . . . Well, let's see. Life appeared in the chemical broth of our ancient oceans about what—five billion years ago?"

"Three and a half or four."

"Okay. Bacteria, microorganisms evolved into higher forms, more complex forms, which evolved into still more complex forms. Life gradually spread to the land. I don't know . . . slimes at the edge of the oceans . . . amphibians. The amphibians moved inland, evolved into reptiles. The reptiles evolved into mammals. This was what? A billion years ago?"

"Only about a quarter of a billion years ago."

"Okay. Anyway, the mammals . . . I don't know. Small critters in small niches—under bushes, in the trees. . . . From the critters in the trees came the primates. Then, I don't know—maybe ten or fifteen million years ago—one branch of the primates left the trees and . . ." I ran out of steam.

"This isn't a test," Ishmael said. "The broad outlines will do—just the story as it's generally known, as it's known by bus drivers and ranch hands and senators."

"Okay," I said, and closed my eyes again. "Okay. Well, one thing led to another. Species followed species, and finally man appeared. That was what? Three million years ago?"

"Three seems pretty safe."

"Okay."

"Is that it?"

"That's it in outline."

"The story of creation as it's told in your culture."

"That's right. To the best of our present knowledge."

Ishmael nodded and told me to turn off the tape recorder. Then he sat back with a sigh that rumbled through the glass like a distant volcano, folded his hands over his central paunch, and gave me a long, inscrutable look. "And you, an intelligent and moderately well-educated person, would have me believe that this isn't a myth."

"What's mythical about it?"

"I didn't say there was anything mythical *about* it. I said it was a myth."

I think I laughed nervously. "Maybe I don't know what you mean by a myth."

"I don't mean anything you don't mean. I'm using the word in the ordinary sense."

"Then it's not a myth."

"Certainly it's a myth. Listen to it." Ishmael told me to rewind the tape and play it back.

After listening to it, I sat there looking thoughtful for a minute or two, for the sake of appearances. Then I said, "It's not a myth. You could put that in an eighth-grade science text, and I don't think there's a school board anywhere that would quibble with it—leaving aside the Creationists."

"I agree wholeheartedly. Haven't I said that the story is ambient in your culture? Children assemble it from many media, including science textbooks."

"Then what are you saying? Are you trying to tell me that this isn't a factual account?"

"It's full of facts, of course, but their arrangement is purely mythical."

"I don't know what you're talking about."

"You've obviously turned off your mind. Mother Culture has crooned you to sleep."

I gave him a hard look. "Are you saying that evolution is a myth?"

"No."

"Are you saying that man did not evolve?"

"No."

"Then what is it?"

Ishmael looked at me with a smile. Then he shrugged his shoulders. Then he raised his eyebrows.

I stared at him and thought: *I'm being teased by a gorilla.* It didn't help.

"Play it again," he told me.

When it was over, I said, "Okay, I heard one thing, the word *appeared.* I said that finally man *appeared.* Is that it?"

"No, it's nothing like that. I'm not quibbling over a word. It was clear from the context that the word *appeared* was just a synonym for *evolved.*"

"Then what the hell is it?"

"You're really not thinking, I'm afraid. You've recited a story you've heard a thousand times, and now you're listening to Mother Culture as she murmurs in your ear: 'There, there, my child, there's nothing to think about, nothing to worry about, don't get excited, don't listen to the nasty animal, this is no myth, nothing I tell you is a myth, so there's nothing to think about, nothing to worry about, just listen to my voice and go to sleep, go to sleep, go to sleep. . . .'"

I chewed on a lip for a while, then I said, "That doesn't help."

"All right," he said. "I'll tell you a story of my own, and maybe that'll help." He nibbled for a moment on a leafy wand, closed his eyes, and began.

3

This story (Ishmael said) takes place half a billion years ago—an inconceivably long time ago, when this planet would be all but unrecognizable to you. Nothing at all stirred on the land, except the wind and the dust. Not a single blade of grass waved in the wind, not a single cricket chirped, not a single bird soared in the sky. All these things were tens of millions of years in the future. Even the seas were eerily still and silent, for the vertebrates too were tens of millions of years away in the future.

But of course there was an anthropologist on hand. What sort of world would it be without an anthropologist? He was, however, a very depressed and disillusioned anthropologist, for he'd been everywhere on the planet looking for someone to interview, and every tape in his knapsack was as blank as the sky. But one day as he was moping along beside the ocean he saw what seemed to be a living creature in the shallows off shore. It was nothing to brag about, just a sort of squishy blob, but it was the only prospect he'd seen in all his journeys, so he waded out to where it was bobbing in the waves.

He greeted the creature politely and was greeted in kind, and soon the two of them were good friends. The anthropologist explained as well as he could that he was a student of life-styles and customs, and begged his new friend for information of this sort, which was readily forthcoming. "And now," he said at last, "I'd like to get on tape in your own words some of the stories you tell among yourselves."

"Stories?" the other asked.

"You know, like your creation myth, if you have one."

"What is a creation myth?" the creature asked.

"Oh, you know," the anthropologist replied, "the fanciful tale you tell your children about the origins of the world."

Well, at this, the creature drew itself up indignantly—at least as well as a squishy blob can do—and replied that his people had no such fanciful tale.

"You have no account of creation then?"

"Certainly we have an account of creation," the other snapped. "But it is definitely not a *myth*."

"Oh, certainly not," the anthropologist said, remembering his training at last. "I'll be terribly grateful if you share it with me."

"Very well," the creature said. "But I want you to understand that, like you, we are a strictly rational people, who accept nothing that is not based on observation, logic, and the scientific method."

"Of course, of course," the anthropologist agreed.

So at last the creature began its story. "The universe," it said, "was born a long, long time ago, perhaps ten or fifteen billion years ago. Our own solar system—this star, this planet and all the others—seem to have come into being some two or three billion years ago. For a long time, nothing whatever lived here. But then, after a billion years or so, life appeared."

"Excuse me," the anthropologist said. "You say that life appeared. Where did that happen, according to your myth—I mean, according to your scientific account."

The creature seemed baffled by the question and turned a pale lavender. "Do you mean in what precise spot?"

"No. I mean, did this happen on the land or in the sea?"

"Land?" the other asked. "What is land?"

"Oh, you know," he said, waving toward the shore, "the expanse of dirt and rocks that begins over there."

The creature turned a deeper shade of lavender and said,

"I can't imagine what you're gibbering about. The dirt and rocks over there are simply the lip of the vast bowl that holds the sea."

"Oh yes," the anthropologist said, "I see what you mean. Quite. Go on."

"Very well," the other said. "For many millions of centuries the life of the world was merely microorganisms floating helplessly in a chemical broth. But little by little, more complex forms appeared: single-celled creatures, slimes, algae, polyps, and so on.

"But finally," the creature said, turning quite pink with pride as he came to the climax of his story, "but finally *jellyfish appeared*!"

4

Nothing much came out of me for ninety seconds or so, except maybe waves of baffled fury. Then I said, "That's not fair."

"What do you mean?"

"I don't exactly know what I mean. You've made some sort of point, but I don't know what it is."

"You don't?"

"No, I don't."

"What did the jellyfish mean when it said, 'But finally jellyfish appeared'?"

"It meant . . . that is what it was all leading up to. This is what the whole ten or fifteen billion years of creation were leading up to: jellyfish."

"I agree. And why doesn't *your* account of creation end with the appearance of jellyfish?"

I suppose I tittered. "Because there was more to come beyond jellyfish."

"That's right. Creation didn't end with jellyfish. Still to

come were the vertebrates and the amphibians and the reptiles and the mammals, and of course, finally, man."

"Right."

"And so your account of creation ends, 'And finally man appeared.'"

"Yes."

"Meaning what?"

"Meaning that there was no more to come. Meaning that creation had come to an end."

"This is what it was all leading up to."

"Yes."

"Of course. Everyone in your culture knows this. The pinnacle was reached in man. Man is the climax of the whole cosmic drama of creation."

"Yes."

"When man finally appeared, creation came to an end, because its objective had been reached. There was nothing left to create."

"That seems to be the unspoken assumption."

"It's certainly not always unspoken. The religions of your culture aren't reticent about it. Man is the end product of creation. Man is the creature for whom all the rest was made: this world, this solar system, this galaxy, the universe itself."

"True."

"Everyone in your culture knows that the world wasn't created for jellyfish or salmon or iguanas or gorillas. It was created for man."

"That's right."

Ishmael fixed me with a sardonic eye. "And this is not mythology?"

"Well . . . the facts are facts."

"Certainly. Facts are facts, even when they're embodied in mythology. But what about the rest? Did the entire cosmic process of creation come to an end three million years ago, right here on this little planet, with the appearance of man?"

"No."

"Did even the planetary process of creation come to an end three million years ago with the appearance of man? Did evolution come to a screeching halt just because man had arrived?"

"No, of course not."

"Then why did you tell it that way?"

"I guess I told it that way, because that's the way it's told."

"That's the way it's told among the Takers. It's certainly not the only way it can be told."

"Okay, I see that now. How would you tell it?"

He nodded toward the world outside his window. "Do you see the slightest evidence anywhere in the universe that creation came to an end with the birth of man? Do you see the slightest evidence anywhere out there that man was the climax toward which creation had been straining from the beginning?"

"No. I can't even imagine what such evidence would look like."

"That should be obvious. If the astrophysicists could report that the fundamental creative processes of the universe came to a halt five billion years ago, when our solar system made its appearance, that would offer at least some support for these notions."

"Yes, I see what you mean."

"Or if the biologists and paleontologists could report that speciation came to a halt three million years ago, this too would be suggestive."

"Yes."

"But you know that neither of these things happened in fact. Very far from it. The universe went on as before, the planet went on as before. Man's appearance caused no more stir than the appearance of jellyfish."

"Very true."

Ishmael gestured toward the tape recorder. "So what are we to make of that story you told?"

I bared my teeth in a rueful grin. "It's a myth. Incredibly enough, it's a myth."

5

"I told you yesterday that the story the people of your culture are enacting is about the meaning of the world, about divine intentions in the world, and about human destiny."

"Yes."

"And according to this first part of the story, what is the meaning of the world?"

I thought about that for a moment. "I don't quite see how it explains the meaning of the world."

"Along about the middle of your story, the focus of attention shifted from the universe at large to this one planet. Why?"

"Because this one planet was destined to be the birthplace of man."

"Of course. As you tell it, the birth of man was a central event—indeed *the* central event—in the history of the cosmos itself. From the birth of man on, the rest of the universe ceases to be of interest, ceases to participate in the unfolding drama. For this, the earth alone is sufficient; it is the birthplace and home of man, and that's its meaning. The Takers regard the world as a sort of human life-support system, as a machine designed to produce and sustain human life."

"Yes, that's so."

"In your telling of the story, you naturally left out any mention of the gods, because you didn't want it to be tainted with mythology. Since its mythological character is now established, you no longer have to worry about that. Supposing there is a divine agency behind creation, what can you tell me about the gods' intentions?"

"Well, basically, what they had in mind when they started out was man. They made the universe so that our galaxy could be in it. They made the galaxy so that our solar system could be in it. They made our solar system so that our planet could be in it. And they made our planet so that we could be in it. The whole thing was made so that man would have a hunk of dirt to stand on."

"And this is generally how it's understood in your culture—at least by those who assume that the universe is an expression of divine intentions."

"Yes."

"Obviously, since the entire universe was made so that man could be made, man must be a creature of enormous importance to the gods. But this part of the story gives no hint of their intentions toward him. They must have some special destiny in mind for him, but that's not revealed here."

"True."

6

"Every story is based on a premise, is the *working out* of a premise. As a writer, I'm sure you know that."

"Yes."

"You'll recognize this one: *Two children of warring families fall in love.*"

"Right. *Romeo and Juliet.*"

"The story being enacted in the world by the Takers also has a premise, which is embodied in the part of the story you told me today. See if you can figure out what it is."

I closed my eyes and pretended I was working hard,

when in fact I knew I didn't stand a chance. "I'm afraid I don't see it."

"The story the Leavers have enacted in the world has an entirely different premise, and it would be impossible for you to discover it at this point. But you should be able to discover the premise of your own story. It's a very simple notion and the most powerful in all of human history. Not necessarily the most beneficial but certainly the most powerful. Your entire history, with all its marvels and catastrophes, is a working out of this premise."

"Truthfully, I can't even imagine what you're getting at."

"Think. . . . Look, the world wasn't made for jellyfish, was it?"

"No."

"It wasn't made for frogs or lizards or rabbits."

"No."

"Of course not. The world was made for man."

"That's right."

"Everyone in your culture knows that, don't they? Even atheists who swear there is no god know that the world was made for man."

"Yes, I'd say so."

"All right. That's the premise of your story: *The world was made for man.*"

"I can't quite grasp it. I mean, I can't quite see why it's a premise."

"The people of your culture *made* it a premise—*took* it as a premise. They said: *What if* the world was made for *us*?"

"Okay. Keep going."

"Think of the consequences of taking that as your premise: If the world was made for you, *then what*?"

"Okay, I see what you mean. I think. If the world was made for us, then it *belongs* to us and we can do what we damn well please with it."

"Exactly. That's what's been happening here for the past ten thousand years: You've been doing what you damn well please with the world. And of course you mean to go right on doing what you damn well please with it, because the whole damn thing *belongs to you*."

"Yes," I said, and thought for a second. "Actually, that's pretty amazing. I mean, you hear this fifty times a day. People talk about *our* environment, *our* seas, *our* solar system. I've even heard people talk about *our wildlife*."

"And just yesterday you assured me with complete confidence that there was nothing in your culture remotely resembling mythology."

"True. I did." Ishmael continued to stare at me morosely. "I was wrong," I told him. "What more do you want?"

"Astonishment," he said.

I nodded. "I'm astonished, all right. I just don't let it show."

"I should have gotten you when you were seventeen."

I shrugged, meaning that I wished he had.

7

"Yesterday I told you that your story provides you with an explanation of *how things came to be this way*."

"Right."

"What contribution does this first part of the story make to that explanation?"

"You mean . . . what contribution does it make to explaining how things came to be the way they are right now?"

"That's right."

"Offhand, I don't see how it makes *any* contribution to it."

"Think. Would things have come to be this way if the world had been made for jellyfish?"

"No, they wouldn't."

"Obviously not. If the world had been made for jellyfish, things would be entirely different."

"That's right. But it wasn't made for jellyfish, it was made for man."

"And this partly explains *how things came to be this way.*"

"Right. It's sort of a sneaky way of blaming everything on the gods. If they'd made the world for jellyfish, then none of this would have happened."

"Exactly," Ishmael said. "You're beginning to get the idea."

8

"Do you have a feeling now for where you might find the other parts of this story—the middle and the end?"

I gave this some thought. "I'd watch *Nova,* I think."

"Why?"

"I'd say that if *Nova* was doing the story of creation, the story I told today would be the outline. All I have to do now is figure out how they'd do the rest."

"Then that's your next assignment. Tomorrow I want to hear the middle of the story."

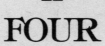

FOUR

1

"Okay," I said. "I think I have the middle and the end of the story down pat."

Ishmael nodded and I started the tape recorder.

"What I did was start with the premise: The world was made for man. Then I asked myself how I would write the story as a treatment for *Nova*. It came out like this:

"The world was made for man, but it took him a long, long time to figure that out. For nearly three million years he lived as though the world had been made for jellyfish.

67

That is, he lived as though he were just like any other creature, as though he were a lion or a wombat."

"What exactly does it mean to live like a lion or a wombat?"

"It means . . . to live at the mercy of the world. It means to live without having any control over your environment."

"I see. Go on."

"Okay. In this condition, man could not be truly man. He couldn't develop a truly human way of life—a way of life that was distinctively human. So, during the early part of his life—actually the greater part of his life—man just foozled along getting nowhere and doing nothing.

"As it happened, there was a key problem to be solved, and it was this that took me a long time to work out: what the problem was. Man could get nowhere living like a lion or a wombat, because if you're a lion or a wombat. . . . In order to accomplish anything, man had to settle down in one place where he could get to work, so to speak. I mean that it was impossible for him to get beyond a certain point living out in the open as a hunter-gatherer, always moving from place to place in search of food. To get beyond that point, he had to settle down, had to have a permanent base from which he could begin to master his environment.

"Okay. Why not? I mean, well, what was stopping him from doing that? What was stopping him was the fact that if he settled down in one place for more than a few weeks, he'd starve. As a hunter-gatherer, he would simply clean the place out—there would be nothing left to hunt and gather. In order to achieve settlement, man had to learn one fundamental manipulation. He had to learn how to manipulate his environment so that this food-exhaustion didn't occur. He had to manipulate it so that it produced *more human food*. In other words, he had to become an agriculturalist.

"This was the turning point. The world had been made for man, but he was unable to take possession of it until this problem was cracked. And he finally cracked it about ten thousand years ago, back there in the Fertile Crescent. This was a very big moment—the biggest in human history up to this point. Man was at last free of all those restraints that. . . . The limitations of the hunting-gathering life had kept man in check for three million years. With agriculture, those limitations vanished, and his rise was meteoric. Settlement gave rise to division of labor. Division of labor gave rise to technology. With the rise of technology came trade and commerce. With trade and commerce came mathematics and literacy and science, and all the rest. The whole thing was under way at last, and the rest, as they say, is history.

"And that's the middle of the story."

2

"Very impressive," Ishmael said. "I'm sure you realize that the 'big moment' you've just described was in fact the birth of your culture."

"Yes."

"It should be pointed out, however, that the notion that agriculture spread across the world from a single point of origin is distinctly old hat. Nevertheless the Fertile Crescent remains the *legendary* birthplace of agriculture, at least in the West, and this has a special importance that we'll look at later on."

"Okay."

"Yesterday's part of the story revealed the meaning of the world as it's understood among the Takers: The world is a human life-support system, a machine designed to produce and sustain human life."

"Right."

"Today's part of the story seems to be about the destiny of

man. Obviously it was not man's destiny to live like a lion or a wombat."

"That's right."

"What is man's destiny then?"

"Hm," I said. "Well. Man's destiny is . . . to achieve, to accomplish great things."

"As it's known among the Takers, man's destiny is more specific than that."

"Well, I suppose you could say that his destiny is to build civilization."

"Think mythologically."

"I'm afraid I don't know how that's done."

"I'll demonstrate. Listen."

I listened.

3

        "As we saw yesterday, creation wasn't complete when jellyfish appeared or when amphibians appeared or when reptiles appeared or even when mammals appeared. According to your mythology, it was complete only when man appeared."

"Right."

"Why was the world and the universe incomplete without man? Why did the world and the universe *need* man?"

"I don't know."

"Well, think about it. Think about the world without man. *Imagine* the world without man."

"Okay," I said, and closed my eyes. A couple minutes later I told him I was imagining the world without man.

"What's it like?"

"I don't know. It's just the world."

"Where are you?"

"What do you mean?"

"Where are you looking at it from?"

"Oh. From above. From outer space."

"What are you doing up there?"

"I don't know."

"Why aren't you down on the surface?"

"I don't know. Without man on it . . . I'm just a visitor, an alien."

"Well, go on down to the surface."

"Okay," I said, but after a minute I went on to say, "That's interesting. I'd rather *not* go down there."

"Why? What's down there?"

I laughed. "The *jungle* is down there."

"I see. You mean, 'Nature, red in tooth and claw . . . Dragons of the prime that tare each other in their slime.'"

"That's it."

"And what would happen if you did go down there?"

"I'd be one of the ones the dragons were tearing in their slime."

I opened my eyes in time to see Ishmael nodding. "And it is at this point that we begin to see where man fits into the divine scheme. The gods didn't mean to leave the world a jungle, did they?"

"You mean in our mythology? Certainly not."

"So: Without man, the world was unfinished, was just nature, red in tooth and claw. It was in chaos, in a state of primeval anarchy."

"That's right. That's it exactly."

"So it needed what?"

"It needed someone to come in and . . . straighten it out. Someone to put it in order."

"And what sort of person is it who straightens things out? What sort of person takes anarchy in hand and puts it in order?"

"Well . . . a ruler. A king."

"Of course. The world needed a ruler. It needed man."

"Yes."

"So now we have a clearer idea what this story is all about:

The world was made for man, and man was made to rule it."

"Yes. That's very obvious now. Everyone understands that."

"And this is what?"

"What?"

"Is this fact?"

"No."

"Then what is it?"

"It's mythology," I said.

"Of which no trace is to be found in your culture."

"That's right."

Once again Ishmael stared at me glumly through the glass.

"Look," I said after a bit. "The things you're showing me, the things you're doing, are . . . almost beyond belief. I know that. But it's just not in me to leap up out of my chair while striking my brow and crying, 'My God, this is incredible!'"

He wrinkled his forehead thoughtfully for a moment before saying: "What's *wrong* with you then?"

He seemed so genuinely concerned that I had to smile.

"All frozen inside," I told him. "An iceberg."

He shook his head, sorry for me.

4

"To return to our subject. . . . As you say, it took man a long, long time to tumble to the fact that he was meant for greater things than he could achieve living like a lion or a wombat. For some three million years he was just part of the anarchy, was just one more creature rolling around in the slime."

"Right."

"It was only about ten thousand years ago that he finally realized that his place was not in the slime. He had to lift himself out of the slime and take this place in hand and straighten it out."

"Right."

"But the world didn't meekly submit to human rule, did it?"

"No."

"No, the world defied him. What man built up, the wind and rain tore down. The fields he cleared for his crops and his villages, the jungle fought to reclaim. The seeds he sowed, the birds snatched away. The shoots he nurtured, the insects nibbled. The harvest he stored, the mice plundered. The animals he bred and fed, the wolves and foxes stole away. The mountains, the rivers, and the oceans stood in their places and would not make way for him. The earthquake, the flood, the hurricane, the blizzard, and the drought would not disappear at his command."

"True."

"The world would not meekly submit to man's rule, so he had to do what to it?"

"What do you mean?"

"If the king comes to a city that will not submit to his rule, what does he have to do?"

"He has to conquer it."

"Of course. In order to make himself the ruler of the world, man first had to conquer it."

"Good lord," I said—and nearly leaped up out of my chair while striking my brow and all the rest.

"Yes?"

"You hear this fifty times a day. You can turn on the radio or the television and hear it every hour. Man is conquering the deserts, man is conquering the oceans, man is conquering the atom, man is conquering the elements, man is conquering outer space."

Ishmael smiled. "You didn't believe me when I said that this story is ambient in your culture. Now you see what I mean. The mythology of your culture hums in your ears so constantly that no one pays the slightest bit of attention to it. Of course man is conquering space and the atom and the deserts and the oceans and the elements. According to your mythology, this is what he was *born* to do."

"Yes. That's very clear now."

5

"Now the first two parts of the story have come together: The world was made for man, and man was made to conquer and rule it. And how does the second part contribute to your explanation of *how things came to be this way*?"

"Let me think about that. . . . Once again this is a sort of sneaky way of blaming the gods. They made the world for man, and they made man to conquer and rule it—which he eventually did. And this is how things came to be the way they are."

"Nail it down. Go a little deeper."

I closed my eyes and gave it a couple of minutes, but nothing came.

Ishmael nodded toward the windows. "All this—all your triumphs and tragedies, all your marvels and miseries—are a direct result of . . . what?"

I chewed on it for a while, but I still couldn't see what he was getting at.

"Try it this way," Ishmael said. "Things wouldn't be the way they are if the gods had meant man to live like a lion or a wombat, would they?"

"No."

"Man's destiny was to conquer and rule the world. So things came to be this way as a direct result of . . . ?"

"Of man fulfilling his destiny."

"Of course. And he *had* to fulfill his destiny, didn't he?"

"Yes, absolutely."

"So what is there to get excited about?"

"Very true, very true."

"As the Takers see it, all this is simply the price of becoming human."

"How do you mean?"

"It wasn't possible to become fully human living beside the dragons in the slime, was it?"

"No."

"In order to become fully human, man had to pull himself out of the slime. And all this is the result. As the Takers see it, the gods gave man the same choice they gave Achilles: a brief life of glory or a long, uneventful life in obscurity. And the Takers chose a brief life of glory."

"Yes, that's certainly how it's understood. People just shrug and say, 'Well, this is the price that had to be paid for indoor plumbing and central heating and air conditioning and automobiles and all the rest.'" I gave him a quizzical look. "And what are *you* saying?"

"I'm saying that the price you've paid is not the price of becoming human. It's not even the price of having the things you just mentioned. It's the price of enacting a story that casts mankind as the enemy of the world."

FIVE

1

"We have the beginning and middle of the story together," Ishmael said when we started the next day. "Man is finally beginning to fulfill his destiny. The conquest of the world is under way. And how does the story end?"

"I guess I should have kept on going yesterday. I've sort of lost the thread."

"Perhaps it would help to listen to the way the second part ends."

"Good idea." I rewound a minute or so of tape and let it play:

"Man was at last free of all those restraints that. . . . The limitations of the hunting-gathering life had kept man in check for three million years. With agriculture, those limitations vanished, and his rise was meteoric. Settlement gave rise to division of labor. Division of labor gave rise to technology. With the rise of technology came trade and commerce. With trade and commerce came mathematics and literacy and science, and all the rest. The whole thing was under way at last, and the rest, as they say, is history."

"Right," I said. "Okay. Man's destiny was to conquer and rule the world, and this is what he's done—almost. He hasn't quite made it, and it looks as though this may be his undoing. The problem is that man's conquest of the world has itself devastated the world. And in spite of all the mastery we've attained, we don't have enough mastery to *stop* devastating the world—or to repair the devastation we've already wrought. We've poured our poisons into the world as though it were a bottomless pit—and we *go on* pouring our poisons into the world. We've gobbled up irreplaceable resources as though they could never run out—and we *go on* gobbling them up. It's hard to imagine how the world could survive another century of this abuse, but nobody's really doing anything about it. It's a problem our children will have to solve, or their children.

"Only one thing can save us. We have to *increase* our mastery of the world. All this damage has come about through our conquest of the world, but we have to *go on* conquering it until our rule is *absolute*. Then, when we're in *complete* control, everything will be fine. We'll have fusion power. No pollution. We'll turn the rain on and off. We'll grow a bushel of wheat in a square centimeter. We'll turn the oceans into farms. We'll control the weather—no more hurricanes, no more tornadoes, no more droughts, no more untimely frosts. We'll make the clouds release their water over the land instead of dumping it uselessly into the oceans. All the life processes of this planet will be where they belong—where the gods meant them to be—in our hands. And we'll manipulate them the way a programmer manipulates a computer.

"And that's where it stands right now. We have to carry the conquest forward. And carrying it forward is either going to destroy the world or turn it into a paradise—into the paradise it was meant to be under human rule.

"And if we manage to do this—if we finally manage to make ourselves the absolute rulers of the world—then nothing can stop us. Then we move into the *Star Trek* era. Man moves out into space to conquer and rule the entire universe. And that may be the ultimate destiny of man: to conquer and rule the entire universe. That's how wonderful man is."

2

To my astonishment, Ishmael picked up a wand from his pile and waved it at me in an enthusiastic gesture of approval. "Once again, that was excellent," he said, neatly biting off its leafy head.

"But you realize, of course, that if you'd been telling this part of the story a hundred years ago—or even fifty years ago—you would have spoken only of the paradise to come. The idea that man's conquest of the world could be anything but beneficial would have been unthinkable to you. Until the last three or four decades, the people of your culture had no doubt that things were just going to go on getting better and better and better forever. There was no conceivable end in sight."

"Yes, that's so."

"There is, however, one element of the story that you've

left out, and we need it to complete your culture's explanation of *how things came to be this way*."

"What element is that?"

"I think you can figure it out. So far we have this much: *The world was made for man to conquer and rule, and under human rule it was meant to become a paradise.* This clearly has to be followed by a 'but.' It has *always* been followed by a 'but.' This is because the Takers have always perceived that the world was far short of the paradise it was meant to be."

"True. Let me see . . . How's this: The world was made for man to conquer and rule, but his conquest turned out to be more destructive than was anticipated."

"You're not listening. The 'but' was part of the story long before your conquest became globally destructive. The 'but' was there to explain all the flaws in your paradise— warfare and brutality and poverty and injustice and corruption and tyranny. It's still there today to explain famine and oppression and nuclear proliferation and pollution. It explained World War II, and if it ever has to, it will explain World War III."

I looked at him blankly.

"This is a commonplace. Any third-grader could supply it."

"I'm sure you're right, but I don't see it yet."

"Come, think. What went wrong here? What has *always* gone wrong here? Under human rule, the world should have become a paradise, but . . ."

"But people screwed it up."

"Of course. And why did they screw it up?"

"Why?"

"Did they screw it up because they didn't *want* a paradise?"

"No. The way it's seen is . . . they were *bound* to screw it up. They wanted to turn the world into a paradise, but, being human, they were bound to screw it up."

"But why? Why, being human, were they bound to screw it up?"

"It's because there's something fundamentally *wrong* with humans. Something that definitely works against paradise. Something that makes people stupid and destructive and greedy and shortsighted."

"Of course. Everyone in your culture knows this. Man was born to turn the world into a paradise, but tragically he was born flawed. And so his paradise has always been spoiled by stupidity, greed, destructiveness, and shortsightedness."

"That's right."

3

Having second thoughts, I gave him a long incredulous stare. "Are you suggesting that this explanation is *false*?"

Ishmael shook his head. "It's pointless to argue with mythology. Once upon a time, the people of your culture believed that man's home was the center of the universe. Man was the reason the universe had been created in the first place, so it made sense that his home should be its capital. The followers of Copernicus didn't argue with this. They didn't point at people and say, 'You're wrong.' They pointed at the heavens and said, 'Look at what's actually *there*.'"

"I'm not sure what you're getting at."

"How did the Takers come to the conclusion that there's something fundamentally wrong with humans? What evidence were they looking at?"

"I don't know."

"I think you're being purposely dense. They were looking at the evidence of human history."

"True."

"And when did human history begin?"

"Well . . . three million years ago."

Ishmael gave me a disgusted look. "Those three million years were only very recently tacked onto human history, as you very well know. Before that, it was universally assumed that human history began when?"

"Well, just a few thousand years ago."

"Of course. In fact, among the people of your culture, it was assumed that the whole of human history was *your* history. No one had the slightest suspicion that human life extended beyond your reign."

"That's so."

"So when the people of your culture concluded that there's something fundamentally wrong with humans, what evidence were they looking at?"

"They were looking at the evidence of their own history."

"Exactly. They were looking at a half of one percent of the evidence, taken from a single culture. Not a reasonable sample on which to base such a sweeping conclusion."

"No."

"There's nothing fundamentally wrong with people. Given a story to enact that puts them in accord with the world, they will live in accord with the world. But given a story to enact that puts them at odds with the world, as yours does, they will live at odds with the world. Given a story to enact in which they are the lords of the world, they will *act* like lords of the world. And, given a story to enact in which the world is a foe to be conquered, they will conquer it like a foe, and one day, inevitably, their foe will lie bleeding to death at their feet, as the world is now."

4

"A few days ago," Ishmael said, "I described your explanation of *how things came to be this way* as a mosaic. What we've looked at so far is only the cartoon of the mosaic—the general outline of the picture. We're not going to fill in the cartoon here. That's something you can easily do for yourself when we're finished."

"Okay."

"However, one major element of the cartoon remains to be sketched in before we go on. . . . One of the most striking features of Taker culture is its passionate and unwavering dependence on prophets. The influence of people like Moses, Gautama Buddha, Confucius, Jesus, and Muhammad in Taker history is simply enormous. I'm sure you're aware of that."

"Yes."

"What makes it so striking is the fact that there is absolutely nothing like this among the Leavers—unless it occurs as a response to some devastating contact with Taker culture, as in the case of Wovoka and the Ghost Dance or John Frumm and the Cargo Cults of the South Pacific. Aside from these, there is no tradition whatever of prophets rising up among the Leavers to straighten out their lives and give them new sets of laws or principles to live by."

"I was sort of vaguely aware of that. I suppose everyone is. I think it's . . . I don't know."

"Go on."

"I think the feeling is, what the hell, who cares about these people? I mean, it's no great surprise that savages have no prophets. God didn't really get interested in mankind until those nice white neolithic farmers came along."

"Yes, that's well perceived. But what I want to look at right now is not the absence of prophets among the Leavers but the enormous influence of prophets among the Takers. Millions have been willing to back their choice of prophet with their very lives. What makes them so important?"

"It's a hell of a good question, but I don't think I know the answer."

"All right, try this. What were the prophets trying to accomplish here? What were they here to do?"

"You said it yourself a minute ago. They were here to straighten us out and tell us how we ought to live."

"Vital information. Worth dying for, evidently."

"Evidently."

"But why? Why do you need *prophets* to tell you how you ought to live? Why do you need *anyone* to tell you how you ought to live?"

"Ah. Okay, I see what you're getting at. We need prophets to tell us how we ought to live, because otherwise we wouldn't know."

"Of course. Questions about how people ought to live always end up becoming religious questions among the Takers—always end up being arguments among the prophets. For example, when abortion began to be legalized in this country, it was initially treated as a purely civil matter. But when people began to have second thoughts about it, they turned to their prophets, and it soon became a religious squabble, with both sides lining up clergy to back them. In the same way, the question of legalizing drugs like heroin and cocaine is now being debated in primarily practical terms—but if it ever becomes a serious possibility, people of a certain turn of mind will undoubtedly begin combing scriptures to see what their prophets have to say on the subject."

"Yes, that's so. This is such an automatic response that people just take it for granted."

"A minute ago you said, 'We need prophets to tell us how we ought to live, because otherwise we wouldn't know.'

Why is that? Why wouldn't you know how to live without your prophets?"

"That's a good question. I'd say it's because . . . Look at the case of abortion. We can *argue about it* for a thousand years, but there's never going to be an argument powerful enough to *end* the argument, because every argument has a counterargument. So it's impossible to *know* what we should do. That's why we need the prophet. The prophet *knows*."

"Yes, I think that's it. But the question remains: Why don't *you* know?"

"I think the question remains because I can't answer it."

"You know how to split atoms, how to send explorers to the moon, how to splice genes, but you don't know how people ought to live."

"That's right."

"Why is that? What does Mother Culture have to say?"

"Ah," I said, and closed my eyes. And after a minute or two: "Mother Culture says it's possible to have *certain* knowledge about things like atoms and space travel and genes, but there's no such thing as certain knowledge about how people should live. It's just not available, and that's why we don't have it."

"I see. And having listened to Mother Culture, what do *you* say?"

"In this case, I have to say that I agree. Certain knowledge about how people ought to live is just not *out there*."

"In other words, the best you can do—since there's nothing 'out there'—is to consult the insides of your heads. That's what's being done in the debate about legalizing drugs. Each side is preparing a case based on what's *reasonable*, and whichever way you actually jump you still won't know whether you did the right thing."

"That's absolutely right. It won't be a question of doing what ought to be done, because there's no way of finding that out. It'll just be a question of taking a vote."

"You're quite sure about all this. There's simply no way to obtain any certain knowledge about how people ought to live."

"Absolutely sure."

"How do you come by this assurance?"

"I don't know. Certain knowledge about how to live is . . . unobtainable in any of the ways we derive certain knowledge. As I say, it's just not *out* there."

"Have any of you ever *looked* out there?"

I snickered.

"Has anyone ever said, 'Well, we have certain knowledge about all these other things, why don't we see if any such knowledge can be found about how to live?' Has anyone ever done that?"

"I doubt it."

"Doesn't that seem strange to you? Considering the fact that this is by far the most important problem mankind has to solve—has ever had to solve—you'd think there would be a whole branch of science devoted to it. Instead, we find that not a single one of you has ever wondered whether any such knowledge is even out there to be obtained."

"We know it's not there."

"In advance of looking, you mean."

"That's right."

"Not a very scientific procedure for such a scientific people."

"True."

5

"We now know two highly important things about people," Ishmael said, "at least according to Taker mythology. One, there's something fundamentally wrong with them, and, two, they have no certain knowledge about how they ought to live—and never will have any. It seems as though there should be a connection between these two things."

"Yes. If people knew how to live, then they'd be able to handle what was wrong with human nature. I mean, knowing how to live would have to include knowing how to live as flawed beings. If it didn't, then it wouldn't be the real McCoy. Do you see what I mean?"

"I think so. In effect, you're saying that if you knew how you ought to live, then the flaw in man could be controlled. If you knew how you ought to live, you wouldn't be forever screwing up the world. Perhaps in fact the two things are actually one thing. Perhaps the flaw in man is exactly this: that he doesn't know how he ought to live."

"Yes, there's something to that."

6

"We now have in place all the major elements of your culture's explanation of *how things came to be this way*. The world was given to man to turn into a paradise, but he's always screwed it up, because he's fundamentally flawed. He might be able to do something about this if he knew how he ought to live, but he doesn't—and he never will, because no knowledge about that is obtainable. So, however hard man might labor to turn the world into a paradise, he's probably just going to go on screwing it up."

"Yes, that's the way it seems."

"It's a sorry story you have there, a story of hopelessness and futility, a story in which there is literally *nothing to be done*. Man is flawed, so he keeps on screwing up what should be paradise, and there's nothing you can do about it. You don't know how to live so as to *stop* screwing up paradise, and there's nothing you can do about that. So there you are, rushing headlong toward catastrophe, and all you can do is watch it come."

"Yes, that's the way it seems."

"With nothing but this wretched story to enact, it's no wonder so many of you spend your lives stoned on drugs or booze or television. It's no wonder so many of you go mad or become suicidal."

"True. But is there another one?"

"Another what?"

"Another story to be in."

"Yes, there is another story to be in, but the Takers are doing their level best to destroy that along with everything else."

7

"Have you done much sightseeing in your travels?"

I blinked at him stupidly. "Sightseeing?"

"Have you gone out of your way to have a look at the local sights?"

"I guess so. Sometimes."

"I'm sure you've noticed that *only* tourists really look at local landmarks. For all practical purposes, these landmarks are invisible to the natives, simply because they're always there in plain sight."

"Yes, that's so."

"This is what we've been doing in our journey so far. We've been wandering around your cultural homeland looking at the landmarks the natives never see. A visitor from another planet would find them remarkable, even extraordinary, but the natives of your culture take them for granted and don't even notice them."

"That's right. You've had to clamp my head between your hands and point it in one direction and say, 'Don't you *see* that?' And I'd say, 'See what? There's nothing there to see.'"

"We've spent a lot of today looking at one of your most impressive monuments—an axiom stating that there is no way to obtain any certain knowledge about how people ought to live. Mother Culture offers this for acceptance on its own merits, without proof, since it is inherently unprovable."

"True."

"And the conclusion you draw from this axiom is . . . ?"

"Therefore there's no point in looking for such knowledge."

"That's right. According to your maps, the world of thought is coterminous with your culture. It ends at the border of your culture, and if you venture beyond that border, you simply fall off the edge of the world. Do you see what I mean?"

"I think so."

"Tomorrow we'll screw up our courage and cross that border. And as you'll see, we will not fall off the edge of the world. We'll just find ourselves in new territory, in territory never explored by anyone in your culture, because your maps say it isn't there—and indeed *can't* be there."

SIX

1

"And how are you feeling today?" Ishmael asked. "Palms sweating? Heart going pit-a-pat?"

I gazed at him thoughtfully through the glass that separated us. This twinkle-eyed playfulness was something new, and I wasn't sure I liked it. I was tempted to remind him that he was a *gorilla,* for God's sake, but I held it in and muttered:

"Relatively calm, so far."

"Good. Like the Second Murderer, you are one whom

the vile blows and buffets of the world have so incens'd that you are reckless what you do to spite the world."

"Absolutely."

"Then let's begin. We confront a wall at the boundary of thought in your culture. Yesterday I called it a monument, but I suppose there's nothing to prevent a wall from being a monument as well. In any case, this wall is an axiom stating that certain knowledge about how people should live is unobtainable. I reject this axiom and climb over the wall. We don't need prophets to tell us how to live; we can find out for ourselves by consulting *what's actually there*."

There was nothing to say to that, so I just shrugged.

"You're skeptical, of course. According to the Takers, all sorts of useful information can be found in the universe, but none of it pertains to how people should live. By studying the universe, you've learned how to fly, split atoms, send messages to the stars at the speed of light, and so on, but there's no way of studying the universe to acquire the most basic and needful knowledge of all: the knowledge of how you ought to live."

"That's right."

"A century ago the would-be aeronauts of the world were in exactly the same condition with regard to learning how to fly. Do you see why?"

"No. I don't see what aeronauts have to do with it."

"It was far from certain that the knowledge these would-be aeronauts were looking for existed at all. Some said it wasn't out there to be found, so there was no point in looking for it. Do you see the similarity now?"

"Yes, I suppose."

"There's more to the similarity than that, however. At that point in time, there wasn't a single piece of knowledge about flying that could be considered certain. Everyone had his own theory. One would say, 'The only way to achieve flight is to imitate the bird; you've got to have a pair of flapping wings.' Another would say, 'One pair isn't enough, you've got to have two.' And another would say, 'Nonsense. Paper airplanes fly without flapping wings; you need a pair of rigid wings and a power plant to push you through the air.' And so on. They could argue their pet notions to their hearts' content, because there wasn't a single thing that was certain. All they could do was proceed by trial and error."

"Uh huh."

"What would have enabled them to proceed in a more efficient way?"

"Well, as you say, obviously some knowledge."

"But what knowledge in particular?"

"Lord . . . They needed to know how to produce lift. They needed to know that air flowing over an airfoil . . ."

"What is it you're trying to describe?"

"I'm trying to describe what happens when air flows over an airfoil."

"You mean what *always* happens when air flows over an airfoil?"

"That's right."

"What's that called? A statement that describes what always happens when certain conditions are met."

"A law."

"Of course. The early aeronauts had to proceed by trial and error, because they didn't know the laws of aerodynamics—didn't even know there *were* laws."

"Okay, I see what you're getting at now."

"The people of your culture are in the same condition when it comes to learning how they ought to live. They have to proceed by trial and error, because they don't know the relevant laws—and don't even know that there *are* laws."

"And I agree with them," I said.

"You're certain that no laws can be discovered concerning how people ought to live."

"That's right. Obviously there are made-up laws, like the laws against drug use, but these can be changed by a vote.

You can't change the laws of aerodynamics by a vote—and there are no laws like that about how people should live."

"I understand. That's what Mother Culture teaches, and in this case you agree with her. That's fine. But at last you have a clear understanding of what I'm attempting here: to show you a law that you will agree is not subject to change by any vote."

"Okay. My mind is open, but I can't imagine any way in the world you're going to accomplish that."

2

"What's the law of gravity?" Ishmael asked, once again startling me with an apparent change of subject.

"The law of gravity? Well, the law of gravity is . . . every particle in the universe is attracted to every other particle, and this attraction varies with the distance between them."

"And that expression of the law was read where?"

"What do you mean?"

"It was derived by looking at what?"

"Well . . . at matter, I suppose. The behavior of matter."

"It wasn't derived by a close study of the habits of bees."

"No."

"If you want to understand the habits of bees, you study bees, you don't study mountain-building."

"That's right."

"And if you had the strange notion that there might be a set of laws about how to live, where would you look for it?"

"I don't know."

"Would you look into the heavens?"

"No."

"Would you delve into the realm of subatomic particles?"

"No."

"Would you study the properties of wood?"

"No."

"Take a wild guess."

"Anthropology?"

"Anthropology is a field of study, like physics. Did Newton discover the law of gravity by reading a book on physics? Is that where the law was written?"

"No."

"Where was it written?"

"In matter. In the universe of matter."

"So, again: If there is a law pertaining to life, where will we find it written?"

"I suppose in human behavior."

"I have amazing news for you. Man is *not alone on this planet*. He is part of a community, upon which he depends absolutely. Have you ever had any suspicions to that effect?"

It was the first time I'd seen him raise a single eyebrow.

"You don't have to be sarcastic," I told him.

"What's the name of this community, of which man is only one member?"

"The community of life."

"Bravo. Does it seem at all plausible to you that the law we're looking for could be written in this community?"

"I don't know."

"What does Mother Culture say?"

I closed my eyes and listened for a while. "Mother Culture says that if there were such a law it wouldn't apply to us."

"Why not?"

"Because we're so far above all the rest of that community."

"I see. And can you think of any other laws from which you are exempt because you're humans?"

"What do you mean?"

"I mean that cows and cockroaches are subject to the law of gravity. Are you exempt?"

"No."

"Are you exempt from the laws of aerodynamics?"

"No."

"Genetics?"

"No."

"Thermodynamics?"

"No."

"Can you think of any laws at all from which humans are exempt?"

"Not offhand."

"Let me know if you do. That will be real news."

"Okay."

"But meanwhile, if there does happen to be a law that governs behavior in the community of life in general, humans would be exempt from it."

"Well, that's what Mother Culture says."

"And what do you say?"

"I don't know. I don't see how a law for turtles and butterflies could be of much relevance to us. I assume that turtles and butterflies follow the law you're talking about."

"That's right, they do. As to relevance, the laws of aerodynamics weren't always relevant to you, were they?"

"No."

"When did they become relevant?"

"Well . . . when we wanted to fly."

"When you want to fly, the laws governing flight become relevant."

"Yes, that's right."

"And when you're on the brink of extinction and want to live for a while longer, the laws governing life might conceivably become relevant."

"Yes, I suppose they might."

3

"What's the effect of the law of gravity? What's gravity good for?"

"I'd say that gravity is what organizes things on the macroscopic level. It's what keeps things together—the solar system, the galaxy, the universe."

Ishmael nodded. "And the law we're looking for is the law that keeps the living community together. It organizes things on the biological level just the way the law of gravity organizes things on the macroscopic level."

"Okay." I guess Ishmael could sense I had something else on my mind, because he waited for me to go on. "It's hard to believe our own biologists aren't aware of this law."

Lines of amused astonishment crinkled the blue-gray skin of his face. "Do you imagine that Mother Culture doesn't talk to your biologists?"

"No."

"Then what does she tell them?"

"That if there is such a law it doesn't apply to us."

"Of course. But that doesn't really answer your question. Your biologists would certainly not be astounded to hear that behavior in the natural community follows certain patterns. You have to remember that when Newton articulated the law of gravity, no one was astounded. It's not a superhuman achievement to notice that unsupported objects fall toward the center of the earth. Everyone past the age of two knows that. Newton's achievement was not in discovering the *phenomenon* of gravity, it was in formulating the phenomenon *as a law*."

"Yes, I see what you mean."

"In the same way, nothing you discover here about life in the community of life is going to astound anyone, certainly not naturalists or biologists or animal behaviorists. My achievement, if I succeed, will simply be in formulating it *as a law*."

"Okay. Got it."

4

"Would you say that the law of gravity is about flight?"

I thought about that for a while and said, "It isn't *about* flight, but it's certainly relevant to flight, inasmuch as it applies to aircraft in the same way it applies to rocks. It makes no distinction between aircraft and rocks."

"Yes. That's well said. The law we're looking for here is much like that with respect to civilizations. It's not about civilizations, but it applies to civilizations in the same way that it applies to flocks of birds and herds of deer. It makes no distinction between human civilizations and beehives. It applies to all species without distinction. This is one reason why the law has remained undiscovered in your culture. According to Taker mythology, man is by definition a biological exception. Out of all the millions of species, only one is an *end product*. The world wasn't made to produce frogs or katydids or sharks or grasshoppers. It was made to produce man. Man therefore stands alone, unique and infinitely apart from all the rest."

"True."

5

Ishmael spent the next few minutes staring at a point about twenty inches in front of his nose, and I began to wonder if he'd forgotten I was there. Then he shook his head and came to. For the first time in our acquaintance, he delivered something like a minilecture.

"The gods have played three dirty tricks on the Takers,"

he began. "In the first place, they didn't put the world where the Takers thought it belonged, in the center of the universe. They really hated hearing this, but they got used to it. Even if man's home was stuck off in the boondocks, they could still believe he was the central figure in the drama of creation.

"The second of the gods' tricks was worse. Since man was the climax of creation, the creature for whom all the rest was made, they should have had the decency to produce him in a manner suited to his dignity and importance—in a separate, special act of creation. Instead they arranged for him to evolve from the common slime, just like ticks and liver flukes. The Takers *really* hated hearing this, but they're beginning to adjust to it. Even if man evolved from the common slime, it's still his divinely appointed destiny to rule the world and perhaps even the universe itself.

"But the last of the gods' tricks was the worst of all. Though the Takers don't know it yet, the gods did not exempt man from the law that governs the lives of grubs and ticks and shrimps and rabbits and mollusks and deer and lions and jellyfish. They did not exempt him from this law any more than they exempted him from the law of gravity, and this is going to be the bitterest blow of all to the Takers. To the gods' other dirty tricks, they could adjust. To this one, no adjustment is possible."

He sat there for a while, a hillside of fur and flesh, I guess letting this pronouncement sink in. Then he went on. "Every law has effects or it wouldn't be discoverable as a law. The effects of the law we're looking for are very simple. Species that live in compliance with the law live forever—environmental conditions permitting. This will, I hope, be taken as good news for mankind in general, because if mankind lives in compliance with this law, then it too will live forever—or for as long as conditions permit.

"But of course this isn't the law's only effect. Those species that do *not* live in compliance with the law become extinct. In the scale of biological time, they become extinct very rapidly. And this is going to be very bad news for the people of your culture—the worst they've ever heard."

"I hope," I said, "that you don't think any of this is showing me where to look for this law."

Ishmael thought for a moment, then took a branch from the pile at his right, held it up for me to see, then let it fall to the floor. "That's the effect Newton was trying to explain." He waved a hand toward the world outside. "That's the effect *I'm* trying to explain. Looking out there, you see a world full of species that, environmental conditions permitting, are going to go on living indefinitely."

"Yes, that's what I assume. But why does it need explaining?"

Ishmael selected another branch from his pile, held it up, and let it fall to the floor. "Why does *that* need explaining?"

"Okay. So you're saying this phenomenon is not the result of *nothing*. It's the effect of a law. A law is in operation."

"Exactly. A law is in operation, and my task is to show you how it operates. At this point, the easiest way to show you how it operates is by analogy with laws you already know—the law of gravity and the laws of aerodynamics."

"Okay."

6

"You know that, as we sit here, we are in no sense defying the law of gravity. Unsupported objects fall toward the center of the earth, and the surfaces on which we're sitting are our supports."

"Right."

"The laws of aerodynamics don't provide us with a way of defying the law of gravity. I'm sure you understand that. They simply provide us with a way of using the air as a support. A man sitting in an airplane is subject to the law of gravity in exactly the way we're subject to it sitting here. Nevertheless the man sitting in the plane obviously enjoys a freedom we lack: the freedom of the air."

"Yes."

"The law we're looking for is like the law of gravity: There is no escaping it, but there is a way of achieving the equivalent of flight—the equivalent of freedom of the air. In other words, it is possible to build a civilization that flies."

I stared at him for a while, then I said, "Okay."

"You remember how the Takers went about trying to achieve powered flight. They didn't begin with an understanding of the laws of aerodynamics. They didn't begin with a theory based on research and carefully planned experimentation. They just built contraptions, pushed them off the sides of cliffs, and hoped for the best."

"True."

"All right. I want to follow one of those early trials in detail. Let's suppose that this trial is being made in one of those wonderful pedal-driven contraptions with flapping wings, based on a mistaken understanding of avian flight."

"Okay."

"As the flight begins, all is well. Our would-be airman has been pushed off the edge of the cliff and is pedaling away, and the wings of his craft are flapping like crazy. He's feeling wonderful, ecstatic. He's experiencing the freedom of the air. What he doesn't realize, however, is that this craft is aerodynamically incapable of flight. It simply isn't in compliance with the laws that make flight possible—but he would laugh if you told him this. He's never heard of such laws, knows nothing about them. He would point at those flapping wings and say, 'See? Just like a bird!' Nevertheless, whatever he thinks, he's not in flight. He's an unsupported object falling toward the center of the earth. He's not in flight, he's in free fall. Are you with me so far?"

"Yes."

"Fortunately—or, rather, unfortunately for our airman—he chose a very high cliff to launch his craft from. His disillusionment is a long way off in time and space. There he is in free fall, feeling wonderful and congratulating himself on his triumph. He's like the man in the joke who jumps out of a ninetieth-floor window on a bet. As he passes the tenth floor, he says to himself, 'Well, so far so good!'

"There he is in free fall, experiencing the exhilaration of what he takes to be flight. From his great height he can see for miles around, and one thing he sees puzzles him: The floor of the valley is dotted with craft just like his—not crashed, simply abandoned. 'Why,' he wonders, 'aren't these craft in the air instead of sitting on the ground? What sort of fools would abandon their aircraft when they could be enjoying the freedom of the air?' Ah well, the behavioral quirks of less talented, earthbound mortals are none of his concern. However, looking down into the valley has brought something else to his attention. He doesn't seem to be maintaining his altitude. In fact, the earth seems to be rising up toward him. Well, he's not very worried about that. After all, his flight has been a complete success up to now, and there's no reason why it shouldn't go on being a success. He just has to pedal a little harder, that's all.

"So far so good. He thinks with amusement of those who predicted that his flight would end in disaster, broken bones, and death. Here he is, he's come all this way, and he hasn't even gotten a bruise, much less a broken bone. But then he looks down again, and what he sees really disturbs him. The law of gravity is catching up to him at the rate of thirty-two feet per second per second—at an accelerating rate. The ground is now rushing up toward him in an alarming way. He's disturbed but far from desperate. 'My craft has brought me *this* far in safety,' he tells himself. 'I just have to keep going.' And so he starts pedaling with all his might. Which of course does him no good at all, because his craft simply isn't in accord with the laws of aerodynamics. Even if he had the power of a thousand men in his legs—ten thousand, a million—that craft is not going to achieve flight. That craft is doomed—and so is he unless he abandons it."

"Right. I see what you're saying, but I don't see the connection with what we're talking about here."

Ishmael nodded. "Here is the connection. Ten thousand years ago, the people of your culture embarked on a similar flight: a civilizational flight. Their craft wasn't designed according to any theory at all. Like our imaginary airman, they were totally unaware that there is a law that must be complied with in order to achieve civilizational flight. They didn't even wonder about it. They wanted the freedom of the air, and so they pushed off in the first contraption that came to hand: the Taker Thunderbolt.

"At first all was well. In fact, all was terrific. The Takers were pedaling away and the wings of their craft were flapping beautifully. They felt wonderful, exhilarated. They were experiencing the freedom of the air: freedom from restraints that bind and limit the rest of the biological community. And with that freedom came marvels—all the things you mentioned the other day: urbanization, technology, literacy, mathematics, science.

"Their flight could never end, it could only go on becoming more and more exciting. They couldn't know, couldn't even have guessed that, like our hapless airman, they were in the air but not in flight. They were in free fall, because their craft was simply not in compliance with the law that makes flight possible. But their disillusionment is far away in the future, and so they're pedaling away and having a wonderful time. Like our airman, they see strange sights in the course of their fall. They see the remains of craft very like their own—not destroyed, merely abandoned—by the Maya, by the Hohokam, by the Anasazi, by the peoples of the Hopewell cult, to mention only a few of those found here in the New World. 'Why,' they wonder, 'are these craft on the ground instead of in the air? Why would any people prefer to be earthbound when they could have the freedom of the air, as we do?' It's beyond comprehension, an unfathomable mystery.

"Ah well, the vagaries of such foolish people are nothing to the Takers. They're pedaling away and having a wonderful time. They're not going to abandon *their* craft. They're going to enjoy the freedom of the air forever. But alas, a law is catching up to them. They don't know such a law even exists, but this ignorance affords them no protection from its effects. This is a law as unforgiving as the law of gravity, and it's catching up to them in exactly the same way the law of gravity caught up to our airman: *at an accelerating rate*.

"Some gloomy nineteenth-century thinkers, like Robert Wallace and Thomas Robert Malthus, look down. A thousand years before, even five hundred years before, they would probably have noticed nothing. But now what they see alarms them. It's as though the ground is rushing up to meet them—as though they are going to crash. They do some figuring and say, 'If we go on this way, we're going to be in big trouble in the not-too-distant future.' The other Takers shrug their predictions off. 'We've come all this enormous way and haven't even received so much as a scratch. It's true the ground seems to be rising up to meet us, but that just means we'll have to pedal a little harder. Not to worry.' Nevertheless, just as was predicted, famine soon becomes a routine condition of life in many parts of the Taker Thunderbolt—and the Takers have to pedal even harder and more efficiently than before. But oddly enough, the harder and more efficiently they pedal, the worse conditions become. Very strange. Peter Farb calls it a paradox: 'Intensification of production to feed an increased population leads to a still greater increase in population.' 'Never mind,' the Takers said. 'We'll just have to put some people pedaling away on a reliable method of birth control. Then the Taker Thunderbolt will fly forever.'

"But such simple answers aren't enough to reassure the people of your culture nowadays. Everyone is looking down, and it's obvious that the ground is rushing up toward you—and rushing up faster every year. Basic ecological and planetary systems are being impacted by the Taker Thunderbolt, and that impact increases in intensity every year. Basic, irreplaceable resources are being devoured every year—and they're being devoured more greedily every year. Whole species are disappearing as a result of your encroachment—and they're disappearing in greater numbers every year. Pessimists—or it may be that they're realists—look down and say, 'Well, the crash may be twenty years off or maybe as much as fifty years off. Actually it could happen anytime. There's no way to be sure.' But of course there are optimists as well, who say, 'We must have faith in our craft. After all, it has brought us *this* far in safety. What's ahead isn't doom, it's just a little hump that we can clear if we all just pedal a little harder. Then we'll soar into a glorious, endless future, and the Taker Thunderbolt will take us to the stars and we'll conquer the universe itself.' But your craft isn't going to save you. Quite the contrary, it's your craft that's carrying you toward catastrophe. Five billion of you pedaling away—or ten billion or twenty billion—can't make it fly. It's been in free fall from the beginning, and that fall is about to end."

At last I had something of my own to add to this. "The worst part of it is this," I said, "that the survivors, if there are any, will immediately set about doing it all over again, exactly the same way."

"Yes, I'm afraid you're right. Trial and error isn't a bad way to learn how to build an aircraft, but it can be a disastrous way to learn how to build a civilization."

SEVEN

1

"Here is a puzzle for you to consider," said Ishmael. "You are in a faraway land and find yourself in a strange city isolated from all others. You're immediately impressed by the people you find there. They're friendly, cheerful, healthy, prosperous, vigorous, peaceable, and well educated, and they tell you things have been this way for as long as anyone can remember. Well, you're glad to break your journey here, and one family invites you to stay with them.

"That night you sample their food at dinner and, finding it delicious but unfamiliar, ask them what it is, and they say, 'Oh, it's B meat, of course. That's all we eat.' This naturally puzzles you and you ask if they mean the meat of the little insects that gather honey. They laugh and take you to the window. 'There are some B's there,' they say, pointing to their neighbors in the next house.

"'Good lord!' you exclaim in horror, 'you don't mean that you eat *people*!' And they look at you in a puzzled way and say, 'We eat B's.'

"'How atrocious,' you reply. 'Are they your slaves then? Do you keep them penned up?'

"'Why on earth should we keep them penned up?' your hosts ask.

"'To keep them from running away, of course!'

"By now your hosts are beginning to think you're a little weak in the head, and they explain that the B's would never think of running away, because their own food, the A's, live right across the street.

"Well, I won't weary you with all your outraged exclamations and their baffled explanations. Eventually you piece together the whole ghastly scheme. The A's are eaten by the B's and the B's are eaten by the C's and the C's in turn are eaten by the A's. There is no hierarchy among these food classes. The C's don't lord it over the B's just because the B's are their food, because after all they themselves are the food of the A's. It's all perfectly democratic and friendly. But of course it's all perfectly dreadful to you, and you ask them how they can stand to live in this lawless way. Once again they look at you in bafflement. 'What do you mean, lawless?' they ask. 'We have a law, and we all follow it invariably. This is why we're friendly and cheerful and peaceable and all those other things you find so attractive in us. This law is the foundation of our success as a people and has been so from the beginning.'

"Here at last is the puzzle. Without asking them, how can you discover what law it is they follow?"

I blinked at him for a moment. "I can't imagine."

"Think about it."

"Well . . . obviously their law is that A's eat C's and B's eat A's and C's eat B's."

Ishmael shook his head. "These are food preferences. No law is required."

"I need something more to go on then. All I've got is their food preferences."

"You have three other things to go on. They have a law, they follow it invariably, and because they follow it invariably, they have a highly successful society."

"It's still very tenuous. Unless it's something like . . . 'Be cool.'"

"I'm not asking you to guess what the law is. I'm asking you to devise a method for *discovering* what the law is."

I slid down in my chair, folded my hands on my stomach, and stared at the ceiling. After a few minutes I had an idea. "Is there a penalty for breaking this law?"

"Death."

"Then I'd wait for an execution."

Ishmael smiled. "Ingenious, but hardly a method. Besides, you're overlooking the fact that the law is obeyed invariably. There has never been an execution."

I sighed and closed my eyes. A few minutes later I said: "Observation. Careful observation over a long period."

"That's more like it. What would you be looking for?"

"For what they *didn't* do. For what they *never* did."

"Good. But how would you eliminate irrelevancies? For example, you might find that they never slept standing on their heads or that they never threw rocks at the moon. There would be a million things they never did, but these wouldn't necessarily be prohibited by the law."

"True. Well, let's see. They have a law, they follow it invariably, and according to them . . . ah. According to them, following this law has given them a society that works very well. Am I supposed to take that seriously?"

"Certainly. It's part of the hypothesis."

"Then this would eliminate most of the irrelevancies. The fact that they never sleep standing on their heads wouldn't have anything to do with having a society that works well. Let's see. In effect . . . What I would actually be looking for is . . . I would be closing in on it from two sides. From one side I would be saying: 'What is it that makes this society work?' And from the other side I would be saying: 'What is it they *don't* do that makes this society work?'"

"Bravo. Now, since you've worked this out so brilliantly, I'm going to give you a break: There's going to be an execution after all. For the first time in history, someone has broken the law that is the foundation of their society. They're outraged, horrified, astounded. They take the offender, cut him into little bits, and feed him to the dogs. This should be a big help to you in discovering their law."

"Yes."

"I'll take the part of your host. We've just been to the execution. You may ask questions."

"Okay. Just what did this guy do?"

"He broke the law."

"Yes, but specifically what did he do?"

Ishmael shrugged. "He lived contrary to the law. He did the things we never do."

I glared at him. "That's not fair. You're not answering my questions."

"I tell you the whole sorry tale is public record, young man. His biography, complete in every detail, is available at the library."

I grunted.

"So how are you going to use this biography? It doesn't say how he broke the law. It's just a complete record of how he lived, and much of it is bound to be irrelevant."

"Okay, but I can see that it gives me another guide. I now have three: what makes their society work well, what they never do, and what *he* did that they *never* do."

2

"Very good. These are precisely the three guides you have to the law we're looking for here. The community of life on this planet has worked well for three billion years—has worked beautifully, in fact. The Takers draw back in horror from this community, thinking it to be a place of lawless chaos and savage, relentless competition, where every creature goes in terror of its life. But those of your species who actually live in this community don't find it to be so, and they will fight to the death rather than be separated from it.

"It is in fact an orderly community. The green plants are food for the plant eaters, which are food for the predators, and some of these predators are food for still other predators. And what's left over is food for the scavengers, who return to the earth nutrients needed by the green plants. It's a system that has worked magnificently for billions of years. Filmmakers understandably love footage of gore and battle, but any naturalist will tell you that the species are not in any sense at war with one another. The gazelle and the lion are enemies only in the minds of the Takers. The lion that comes across a herd of gazelles doesn't massacre them, as an enemy would. It kills one, not to satisfy its hatred of gazelles but to satisfy its hunger, and once it has made its kill the gazelles are perfectly content to go on grazing with the lion right in their midst.

"All this comes about because there is a law that is followed invariably within the community, and without this law the community would indeed be in chaos and would very quickly disintegrate and disappear. Man owes his very existence to this law. If the species around him had not obeyed it, he could not have come into being or survived. It's a law that protects not only the community as a whole but species within the community and even individuals. Do you understand?"

"I understand what you're saying, but I have no idea what the law is."

"I'm pointing to its effects."

"Oh. Okay."

"It is the peace-keeping law, the law that keeps the community from turning into the howling chaos the Takers imagine it to be. It's the law that fosters life for all—life for the grasses, life for the grasshopper that feeds on the grasses, life for the quail that feeds on the grasshopper, life for the fox that feeds on the quail, life for the crows that feed on the dead fox.

"The club-finned fish that nosed the shores of the continents came into being because hundreds of millions of generations of life before them had followed this law, and some of them became amphibians following this law. And some of the amphibians became reptiles following this law. And some of the reptiles became birds and mammals following this law. And some of the mammals became primates following this law. And one branch of the primates became *Australopithecus* following this law. And *Australopithecus* became *Homo habilis* following this law. And *Homo habilis* became *Homo erectus* following this law. And *Homo erectus* became *Homo sapiens* following this law. And *Homo sapiens* became *Homo sapiens sapiens* following this law.

"And then about ten thousand years ago one branch of the family of *Homo sapiens sapiens* said, 'Man is exempt from this law. The gods never meant man to be bound by it.' And so they built a civilization that flouts the law at every point, and within five hundred generations—in an eyeblink in the scale of biological time—this branch of the

family of *Homo sapiens sapiens* saw that they had brought
the entire world to the point of death. And their explanation
for this calamity was . . . what?"

"Huh?"

"Man lived harmlessly on this planet for some three
million years, but the Takers have brought the whole thing
to the point of collapse in only five hundred generations.
And their explanation for this is what?"

"I see what you mean. Their explanation is that something is fundamentally wrong with people."

"Not that you Takers may be doing something wrong but
rather that there is something fundamentally wrong with
human nature itself."

"That's right."

"How do you like that explanation now?"

"I'm beginning to have my doubts about it."

"Good."

3

"At the time when the Takers blundered into
the New World and began kicking everything to pieces, the
Leavers here were searching for an answer to this question:
'Is there a way to achieve settlement that is in accord with
the law that we've been following from the beginning of
time?' I don't mean, of course, that they had consciously
formulated this question. They were no more consciously
aware of this law than the early aeronauts were consciously aware of the laws of aerodynamics. But they were
struggling with it all the same: building and abandoning
one civilizational contraption after another, trying to find
one that would fly. Done this way, it's slow work. Proceeding simply by trial and error, it might have taken them
another ten thousand years—or another fifty thousand
years. They apparently had the wisdom to know there was

no hurry. They didn't *have* to get into the air. It made no sense to them to commit themselves to one civilizational craft that was clearly headed for disaster, the way the Takers have done."

Ishmael stopped there, and when he didn't go on, I said, "What now?"

His cheeks crinkled in a smile. "Now you leave and come back when you're prepared to tell me what law or set of laws has been at work in the community of life from the beginning."

"I'm not sure I'm ready for that."

"That's what we've been doing here for the last half week, if not from the very beginning: getting you ready."

"But I wouldn't know where to begin."

"You do know. You have the same three guides as in the case of the A's, the B's, and the C's. The law you're looking for has been obeyed invariably in the living community for three billion years." He nodded to the world outside. "And this is *how things came to be this way*. If this law had not been obeyed from the beginning and in each generation thereafter, the seas would be lifeless deserts and the land would still be dust blowing in the wind. All the countless forms of life that you see here came into being following this law, and following this law, man too came into being. And only once in all the history of this planet has any species tried to live in defiance of this law—and it wasn't an entire species, it was only one people, those I've named Takers. Ten thousand years ago, this one people said, 'No more. Man was not meant to be bound by this law,' and they began to live in a way that flouts the law at every point. Every single thing that is prohibited under the law they incorporated into their civilization *as a fundamental policy*. And now, after five hundred generations, they are about to pay the penalty that any other species would pay for living contrary to this law."

Ishmael turned over a hand. "That should be guide enough for you."

4

The door closed behind me, and there I was. I couldn't go back in and I didn't want to go home, so I just stood there. My mind was a blank. I felt depressed. On no rational grounds, I even managed to feel rejected.

Things were piling up at home. I was falling behind in my work, missing deadlines. In addition, I now had an assignment from Ishmael that did not fill me with enthusiasm. It was time to buckle down and get serious, so I did something I seldom do; I went out and had a drink. I needed to talk to someone, and solitary drinkers are lucky in this regard—they always have someone to talk to.

So: What was at the bottom of these mysterious feelings of depression and rejection? And why had they emerged on this one day in particular? The answer: On this one day in particular, Ishmael had sent me away to work on my own. He might have spared me the investigation I was about to undertake, but he chose not to. Therefore: rejection, of a sort. Childish, of course, to perceive it this way, but I never claimed to be perfect.

There was more to it than this, however, because I still felt depressed. A second bourbon helped me to it: I was making progress. That's right. This was the source of my feeling of depression.

Ishmael had a curriculum. Well, of course, why wouldn't he? He'd developed his curriculum over a period of years, working with one pupil after another. Makes sense. You've got to have a plan. You start here, move to this point, then to this point, this point, and this point, and then, voila! One fine day you're finished. Thanks for your attention, have a nice life, and close the door behind you when you leave.

How far along was I, at this point? Halfway? A third of the

way? A quarter? Whatever, every advance I made took me a step closer to being out of Ishmael's life.

What's the best bad word that describes this way of taking the situation? Selfishness? Possessiveness? Stinginess? Whatever it is, I'll own to it and make no excuses.

I had to face it: I didn't just want a teacher—I wanted a teacher for life.

EIGHT

1

The search for the law took me four days.

I spent one day telling myself I couldn't do it, two days doing it, and one day making sure I'd done it. On the fifth day I went back. As I walked into Ishmael's office, I was mentally rehearsing what I was going to say, which was, "I think I see why you insisted I do it myself."

I looked up from my thoughts and was momentarily disoriented. I had forgotten what was waiting for me there:

the empty room, the lone chair, the slab of glass with a pair of glowing eyes behind it. I quavered a hello into the air.

Then Ishmael did something he'd never done before. By way of greeting, he lifted his upper lip to give me a look at a row of amber teeth as massive as elbows. I scurried to my chair and waited like a schoolboy for his nod.

"I think I see why you insisted I do it myself," I told him. "If you had done the work for me and pointed out the things the Takers do that are never done in the natural community, I would have said, 'Well, sure, so what, big deal.'"

Ishmael grunted.

"Okay. As I make it out, there are four things the Takers do that are never done in the rest of the community, and these are all fundamental to their civilizational system. First, they exterminate their competitors, which is something that never happens in the wild. In the wild, animals will defend their territories and their kills and they will invade their competitors' territories and preempt their kills. Some species even include competitors among their prey, but they never hunt competitors down just to make them dead, the way ranchers and farmers do with coyotes and foxes and crows. What they hunt, they eat."

Ishmael nodded. "Although what you say is true, it should be noted that animals will also kill in self-defense, or even when they merely feel threatened. For example, baboons may attack a leopard that hasn't attacked them. The point to see, however, is that, though baboons will go looking for food, they'll never go looking for leopards."

"I'm not sure I see what you mean."

"I mean that in the absence of food, baboons will organize themselves to find a meal, but in the absence of leopards they will never organize themselves to find a leopard. In other words, it's as you say: when animals go hunting—even extremely aggressive animals like baboons—it's to obtain food, not to exterminate competitors or even animals that prey on them."

"Yes, I see what you're getting at now."

"And how can you be sure this law is invariably followed? I mean, aside from the fact that competitors are never in fact observed to be exterminating each other, in what you call the wild."

"If it weren't invariably followed, then, as you say, things would not have come to be this way. If competitors hunted each other down just to make them dead, then there would *be* no competitors. There would simply be one species at each level of competition: the strongest."

"Go on."

"Next, the Takers systematically destroy their competitors' food to make room for their own. Nothing like this occurs in the natural community. The rule there is: Take what you need, and leave the rest alone."

Ishmael nodded.

"Next, the Takers deny their competitors access to food. In the wild, the rule is: You may deny your competitors access to what you're eating, but you may not deny them access to food in general. In other words, you can say, 'This gazelle is mine,' but you can't say, '*All* the gazelles are mine.' The lion defends its kill as its own, but it doesn't defend the herd as its own."

"Yes, that's true. But suppose you raised up a herd of your own, from scratch, so to speak. Could you defend that herd as your own?"

"I don't know. I suppose so, so long as it wasn't your policy that all the herds in the world were your own."

"And what about denying competitors access to what you're growing?"

"Again . . . *Our* policy is: Every square foot of this planet belongs to us, so if we put it all under cultivation, then all our competitors are just plain out of luck and will have to become extinct. Our policy is to deny our competitors access to *all the food in the world,* and that's obviously something no other species does."

"Bees will deny you access to their hive in the apple tree, but they won't deny you access to the apples."

"That's right."

"Good. And you say there's a fourth thing the Takers do that is never done in the wild, as you call it."

"Yes. In the wild, the lion kills a gazelle and eats it. It doesn't kill a second gazelle to save for tomorrow. The deer eats the grass that's there. It doesn't cut the grass down and save it for the winter. But these are things the Takers do."

"You seem less certain about this one."

"Yes, I *am* less certain. There *are* species that store food, like bees, but most don't."

"In this case, you've missed the obvious. Every living creature stores food. Most simply store it in their bodies, the way lions and deer and people do. For others, this would be inadequate to their adaptations, and they must store food externally as well."

"Yes, I see."

"There's no prohibition against food storage as such. There couldn't be, because that's what makes it all work: the green plants store food for the plant eaters, the plant eaters store food for the predators, and so on."

"True. I hadn't thought of it that way."

"Is there anything else the Takers do that is never done in the rest of the community of life?"

"Not that I can see. Not that seems relevant to what makes that community work."

2

"This law that you have so admirably described defines the limits of competition in the community of life. You may compete to the full extent of your capabilities, but you may not hunt down your competitors or destroy their food or deny them access to food. In other words, you may compete but you may not wage war."

"Yes. As you said, it's the peace-keeping law."

"And what's the effect of the law? What does it promote?"

"Well . . . it promotes order."

"Yes, but I'm after something else now. What would have happened if this law had been repealed ten million years ago? What would the community be like?"

"Once again, I'd have to say there would only be one form of life at each level of competition. If all the competitors for the grasses had been waging war on each other for ten million years, I'd have to think an overall winner would have emerged by now. Or maybe there'd be one insect winner, one avian winner, one reptile winner, and so on. The same would be true at all levels."

"So the law promotes what? What's the difference between the community you've just described and the community as it is?"

"I suppose the community I've just described would consist of a few dozen or a few hundred different species. The community as it is consists of millions of species."

"So the law promotes what?"

"Diversity."

"Of course. And what's the good of diversity?"

"I don't know. It's certainly more . . . interesting."

"What's wrong with a global community that consists of nothing but grass, gazelles, and lions? Or a global community that consists of nothing but rice and humans?"

I gazed into space for a while. "I'd have to think that a community like that would be ecologically fragile. It would be highly vulnerable. Any change at all in existing conditions, and the whole thing would collapse."

Ishmael nodded. "Diversity is a survival factor *for the community itself*. A community of a hundred million species can survive almost anything short of total global catastrophe. Within that hundred million will be thousands that could survive a global temperature drop of twenty degrees—which would be a lot more devastating than it sounds. Within that hundred million will be thousands that could survive a global temperature rise of twenty degrees. But a community of a hundred species or a thousand species has almost no survival value at all."

"True. And diversity is exactly what's under attack here. Every day dozens of species disappear as a direct result of the way the Takers compete outside the law."

"Now that you know there's a law involved, does it make a difference in the way you view what's going on?"

"Yes. I no longer think of what we're doing as a blunder. We're not destroying the world because we're clumsy. We're destroying the world because we are, in a very literal and deliberate way, at war with it."

3

"As you've explained, the community of life would be destroyed if all species exempted themselves from the rules of competition laid down by this law. But what would happen if only *one* species exempted itself?"

"You mean other than man?"

"Yes. Of course it would have to possess an almost human cunning and determination. Suppose that you're a hyena. Why should you share the game with those lazy, domineering lions? It happens again and again: You kill a zebra, and a lion comes along, drives you off, and helps himself while you sit around waiting for the leavings. Is that fair?"

"I thought it was the other way around—the lions make the kill and the hyenas do the harassing."

"Lions make their own kills, of course, but they're perfectly content to appropriate someone else's if they can."

"Okay."

"So you're fed up with them. What are you going to do about it?"

"Exterminate the lions."

"And what's the effect of this?"

"Well . . . no more hassles."

"What were the lions living on?"

"The gazelles. The zebras. The game."

"Now the lions are gone. How does this affect you?"

"I see what you're getting at. There's more game for us."

"And when there's more game for you?"

I looked at him blankly.

"All right. I was assuming you knew the ABC's of ecology. In the natural community, whenever a population's food supply increases, that population increases. As that population increases, its food supply decreases, and as its food supply decreases, that population decreases. This interaction between food populations and feeder populations is what keeps everything in balance."

"I *did* know it. I just wasn't thinking."

"Well," Ishmael said with a baffled frown, "think."

I laughed. "Okay. With lions gone, there's more food for us, and our population grows. It grows to the point where game becomes scarce, then it begins to shrink."

"It would in ordinary circumstances, but you've changed those circumstances. You've decided the law of limited competition doesn't apply to hyenas."

"Right. So we kill off our other competitors."

"Don't make me drag it out of you one word at a time. I want you to work it out."

"Okay. Let's see. After we kill off our competitors for the game . . . our population grows until the game begins to get scarce. There are no more competitors to kill off, so we have to increase the game population. . . . I can't see hyenas going in for animal husbandry."

"You've killed off your competitors for the game, but your game has competitors as well—competitors for the grasses. These are your competitors once removed. Kill them off and there'll be more grass for your game."

"Right. More grass for the game means more game, more game means more hyenas, more hyenas means . . . What's left to kill off?"

Ishmael just raised his eyebrows at me.

"There's nothing left to kill off."

"Think."

I thought. "Okay. We've killed off our direct competitors and our competitors once removed. Now we can kill off our competitors twice removed—the plants that compete with the grasses for space and sunlight."

"That's right. Then there will be more plants for your game and more game for you."

"Funny. . . . This is considered almost holy work by farmers and ranchers. Kill off everything you can't eat. Kill off anything that eats what you eat. Kill off anything that doesn't feed what you eat."

"It *is* holy work, in Taker culture. The more competitors you destroy, the more humans you can bring into the world, and that makes it just about the holiest work there is. Once you exempt yourself from the law of limited competition, everything in the world except your food and the food of your food becomes an enemy to be exterminated."

4

"As you see, one species exempting itself from this law has the same ultimate effect as all species exempting themselves. You end up with a community in which diversity is progressively destroyed in order to support the expansion of a single species."

"Yes. You have to end up where the Takers have ended up—constantly eliminating competitors, constantly increasing your food supply, and constantly wondering what you're going to do about the population explosion. How did you put it the other day? Something about increasing food production to feed an increased population."

"'Intensification of production to feed an increased population leads to a still greater increase in population.' Peter Farb said it in *Humankind*."

"You said it was a paradox?"

"No, *he* said it was a paradox."

"Why?"

Ishmael shrugged. "I'm sure he knows that any species in the wild will invariably expand to the extent that its food supply expands. But, as you know, Mother Culture teaches that such laws do not apply to man."

"True."

5

"I have a question," I said. "As we've gone through these things, I keep wondering if agriculture itself is contrary to this law. I mean, it seems contrary to the law by definition."

"It is—if the only definition you have is the Taker definition. But there are others. Agriculture doesn't have to be a war waged on all life that doesn't support your growth."

"I guess my problem is this. The biological community is an economy, isn't it? I mean, if you start taking more for yourself, then there's got to be less for someone else, for some*thing* else. Isn't that so?"

"Yes. But what are you getting at by taking more for yourself? Why do it?"

"Well, this is the basis for settlement. I can't have settlement unless I have agriculture."

"Are you sure that's what you want?"

"What else would I want?"

"Do you want to grow to the point where you can take

over the world and put every square foot of it under cultivation and force everyone alive to be an agriculturalist? You
understand that that's what the Takers have been doing—
and are still doing. That's what their agricultural system is
designed to support: not just settlement—*growth*. Unlim-
ited growth."

"Okay. But all I want is settlement."

"Then you don't have to go to war."

"But the problem remains. If I'm going to achieve settlement, I have to have more than I had before, and that more
has got to come from *somewhere*."

"Yes, that's true, and I see your difficulty. In the first
place, settlement is not by any means a uniquely human
adaptation. Offhand I can't think of any species that is an
absolute nomad. There's always a territory, a feeding
ground, a spawning ground, a hive, a nest, a roost, a lair, a
den, a hole, a burrow. And there are varying degrees of
settlement among animals, and among humans as well.
Even hunter-gatherers aren't absolute nomads, and there
are intermediate states between them and peoples who are
pure agriculturalists. There are hunter-gatherers who practice intensive collection, who collect and store food surpluses that enable them to be a bit more settled. Then there
are semi-agriculturalists who grow a little and gather a lot.
And then there are near-agriculturalists who grow a lot and
gather a little. And so on."

"But this is not getting to the central problem," I said.

"It *is* getting to the central problem, but your vision is
locked on seeing the problem in one way and one way only.
The point you're missing is this: When *Homo habilis* appeared on the scene—when that particular adaptation that
we call *Homo habilis* appeared on the scene—*something*
had to make way for him. I don't mean that some other
species had to become extinct. I mean simply that, with his
very first bite, *Homo habilis* was in competition with *something*. And not with one thing, with a thousand things—

which all had to be diminished in some small degree if *Homo habilis* was going to live. This is true of every single species that ever came into being on this planet."

"Okay. But I still don't see what this has to do with settlement."

"You're not listening. Settlement is a biological adaptation practiced to some degree by *every* species, including the human. And *every* adaptation supports itself in competition with the adaptations around it. In other words, human settlement isn't *against* the laws of competition, it's *subject* to the laws of competition."

"Ah. Yes. Okay, I see it now."

6

"So, what have we discovered here?"

"We've discovered that any species that exempts itself from the rules of competition ends up destroying the community in order to support its own expansion."

"Any species? Including man?"

"Yes, obviously. That's in fact what's happening here."

"So you see that this—at least this—is not some mysterious wickedness peculiar to the human race. It isn't some imponderable flaw in man that has made the people of your culture the destroyers of the world."

"No. The same thing would happen with any species, at least with any species strong enough to bring it off. Provided that every increase in food supply is answered by an increase in population."

"Given an expanding food supply, any population will expand. This is true of any species, including the human. The Takers have been proving this here for ten thousand years. For ten thousand years they've been steadily increasing food production to feed an increased population, and every time they've done this, the population has increased still more."

I sat there for a minute thinking. Then I said, "Mother Culture doesn't agree."

"Certainly not. I'm sure she disagrees most strenuously. What does she say?"

"She says it's within our power to increase food production *without* increasing our population."

"To what end? Why increase food production?"

"To feed the millions who're starving."

"And as you feed them will you extract a promise that they will not reproduce?"

"Well . . . no, that's not part of the plan."

"So what will happen if you feed the starving millions?"

"They'll reproduce and our population will increase."

"Without fail. This is an experiment that has been performed in your culture annually for ten thousand years, with completely predictable results. Increasing food production to feed an increased population results in yet another increase in population. Obviously it has to have this result, and to predict any other is simply to indulge in biological and mathematical fantasies."

"Even so . . ." I thought some more. "Mother Culture says that, if it comes to that, birth control will solve the problem."

"Yes. If you're ever so foolish as to get into a conversation on this subject with some of your friends, you'll find they heave a great sigh of relief when they remember to make this point. 'Whew! Off the hook!' It's like the alcoholic who swears he'll give up drink before it ruins his life. Global population control is always something that's going to happen in the future. It was something that was going to happen in the future when you were three billion in 1960. Now, when you're five billion, it's still something that's going to happen in the future."

"True. Nevertheless, it *could* happen."

"It could indeed—but not as long as you're enacting this particular story. As long as you're enacting this story, you will go on answering famine with increased food production. You've seen the ads for groups sending food to starving peoples around the world?"

"Yes."

"Have you ever seen ads for groups sending contraceptives anywhere?"

"No."

"Never. Mother Culture talks out of both sides of her mouth on this issue. When you say to her *population explosion* she replies *global population control,* but when you say to her *famine* she replies *increased food production.* But as it happens, increased food production is an annual event and global population control is an event that never happens at all."

"True."

"Within your culture as a whole, there is in fact no significant thrust toward global population control. The point to see is that there never *will* be such a thrust so long as you're enacting a story that says the gods made the world for man. For as long as you enact that story, Mother Culture will demand increased food production for today—and promise population control for tomorrow."

"Yes, I can see that. But I have a question."

"Proceed."

"I know what Mother Culture says about famine. What do *you* say?"

"I? I say nothing, except that your species is not exempt from the biological realities that govern all other species."

"But how does that apply to famine?"

"Famine isn't unique to humans. All species are subject to it everywhere in the world. When the population of any species outstrips its food resources, that population declines until it's once again in balance with its resources. Mother Culture says that humans should be exempt from that process, so when she finds a population that has outstripped its resources, she rushes in food from the outside, thus making it a certainty that there will be even more of them to starve in the next generation. Because the population is never allowed to decline to the point at which it can be supported by its own resources, famine becomes a chronic feature of their lives."

"Yes. A few years ago I read a story in the paper about an ecologist who made the same point at some conference on hunger. Boy, did he get jumped on. He was practically accused of being a murderer."

"Yes, I can imagine. His colleagues all over the world understand perfectly well what he was saying, but they have the good sense not to confront Mother Culture with it in the midst of her benevolence. If there are forty thousand people in an area that can only support thirty thousand, it's no kindness to bring in food from the outside to maintain them at forty thousand. That just guarantees that the famine will continue."

"True. But all the same, it's hard just to sit by and watch them starve."

Ishmael rumbled volcanically. "Who said anything about sitting by and watching them starve? If you can move food in, you can also move people out, can't you?"

"Yes, I suppose so."

"Move the ten thousand out to some part of the world where there's an abundance of food. Italy. Hawaii. Switzerland. Nebraska. Oregon. Wales."

"I doubt if that's an idea that would win much support."

"You'd rather exercise your philanthropy by maintaining forty thousand in a state of chronic starvation."

"I'm afraid that's the case."

"So much for benevolence."

"Even so," I said, "I have one more question on this point."

Ishmael nodded me on.

"We increase food production in the U.S. tremendously every year, but our population growth is relatively slight. On the other hand, population growth is steepest in countries with poor agricultural production. This seems to contradict your correlation of food production with population growth."

He shook his head in mild disgust. "The phenomenon as it's observed is this: 'Every increase in food production to feed an increased population is answered by another increase in population.' This says nothing about where these increases occur."

"I don't get it."

"An increase in food production in Nebraska doesn't necessarily produce a population increase in Nebraska. It may produce a population increase somewhere in India or Africa."

"I still don't get it."

"Every increase in food production is answered by an increase in population *somewhere*. In other words, *someone* is consuming Nebraska's surpluses—and if they weren't, Nebraska's farmers would stop producing those surpluses, pronto."

"True," I said, and spent a few moments in thought. "Are you suggesting that First World farmers are fueling the Third World population explosion?"

"Ultimately," he said, "who else is there to fuel it?"

I sat there staring at him.

7

"As you see, I left a book beside your chair," Ishmael said.

It was *The American Heritage Book of Indians*.

"While we're on or near the subject of population control, there's a map of tribal locations there in the front that you may find illuminating." After I'd studied it for a minute, he asked me what I made of it.

"I didn't realize there were so many. So many different peoples."

"Not all of them were there at the same time, but most of them were. What I'd like you to think about is what served to limit their growth."

"How is the map supposed to help?"

"I wanted you to see that this was far from an empty continent. Population control wasn't a luxury, it was a necessity."

"Okay."

"Any ideas?"

"You mean from looking at the map? No, I'm afraid not."

"Tell me this: What do the people of your culture do if they get tired of living in the crowded Northeast?"

"That's easy. They move to Arizona. New Mexico. Colorado. The wide open spaces."

"And how do the Takers in the wide open spaces like that?"

"They don't. They put bumper stickers on their cars that say, 'If you love New Mexico, go back where you came from.'"

"But they don't go back."

"No, they just keep coming."

"Why can't the Takers of these areas stem the flood? Why can't they limit the population growth of the Northeast?"

"I don't know. I don't see how they could."

"So what you have is a gushing wellspring of growth in one part of the country that no one bothers to turn off, because the excess can always flow into the wide open spaces of the West. Yet each of these states has a boundary. Why don't those boundaries keep them out?"

"Because they're just imaginary lines."

"Exactly. All you have to do to transform yourself into an Arizonan is to cross that imaginary line and settle down. But

the point to note is that around each of the Leaver peoples
on that map was a boundary that was definitely not imaginary: a cultural boundary. If the Navajo started feeling
crowded, they couldn't say to themselves, 'Well, the Hopi
have a lot of wide open space. Let's go over there and be
Hopi.' Such a thing would have been unthinkable to them.
In short, New Yorkers can solve their population problems
by becoming Arizonans, but the Navajo couldn't solve
theirs by becoming Hopi. Those cultural boundaries were
boundaries that no one crossed by choice."

"True. On the other hand, the Navajo could cross the
Hopi's *territorial* boundary."

"You mean they could invade Hopi territory. Yes, absolutely. But the point I'm making still stands. If you crossed
over into Hopi territory, they didn't give you a form to fill
out, they killed you. That worked very well. That gave
people a powerful incentive to limit their growth."

"Yes, there is that."

"These were not people limiting their growth for the
benefit of mankind or for the benefit of the environment.
They limited their growth because for the most part this was
easier than going to war with their neighbors. And of course
there were some who made no great effort to limit their
growth, because they had no qualms about going to war
with their neighbors. I don't mean to suggest that this was
the peaceable kingdom of a utopian dream. In a world
where no Big Brother monitors everyone's behavior and
guarantees everyone's property rights, it works well to have
a reputation for fearlessness and ferocity—and you don't
acquire such a reputation by sending your neighbors curt
notes. You want them to know what they'll be in for if they
don't limit their growth and stay in their own territory."

"Yes, I see. They limited each other."

"But not just by erecting uncrossable territorial boundaries. Their cultural boundaries had to be uncrossable too.
The excess population of the Narraganset couldn't just pack

up and move out west to be Cheyenne. The Narraganset had to stay where they were and limit their population."

"Yes. It's another case where diversity seems to work better than homogeneity."

8

"A week ago," Ishmael said, "when we were talking about laws, you said there's only one kind about how people should live—the kind that can be changed by a vote. What do you think now? Can the laws that govern competition in the community be changed by a vote?"

"No. But they're not absolutes, like the laws of aerodynamics. They can be broken."

"Can't the laws of aerodynamics be broken?"

"No. If your plane isn't built according to the law, it doesn't fly."

"But if you push it off a cliff, it stays in the air, doesn't it?"

"For a while."

"The same is true of a civilization that isn't built in accordance with the law of limited competition. It stays in the air for a while, and then it comes down with a crash. Isn't that what the Takers are facing here? A crash?"

"Yes."

"I'll ask the question another way. Are you certain that any species that, as a matter of policy, exempts itself from the law of limited competition will end by destroying the community to support its own expansion?"

"Yes."

"Then what have we discovered here?"

"We've discovered a piece of certain knowledge about how people ought to live. Must live, in fact."

"Knowledge that a week ago you said was unobtainable."

"Yes. But . . ."

"Yes?"

"I don't see how . . . Hold on for a minute."

"Take your time."

"I don't see how to make this a source of knowledge *in general*. I mean, I don't see any way to apply this knowledge in a general way, to other issues."

"Do the laws of aerodynamics show you how to repair damaged genes?"

"No."

"Then what good are they?"

"They're good for . . . They enable us to fly."

"The law we've outlined here enables species to live— enables species to survive, including the human. It won't tell you whether mood-altering drugs should be legalized or not. It won't tell you whether premarital sex is good or bad. It won't tell you whether capital punishment is right or wrong. It *will* tell you how you have to live if you want to avoid extinction, and that's the first and most fundamental knowledge anyone needs."

"True. All the same . . ."

"Yes?"

"All the same, people will not accept it."

"You mean they won't accept what you've learned here."

"That's right."

"Let's be clear about what they will and will not accept. The law itself is beyond argument. It's there, plainly in place in the community of life. What the Takers will deny is that it applies to mankind."

"That's right."

"That hardly comes as a surprise. Mother Culture could accept the fact that mankind's home is not the center of the universe. She could accept the fact that man evolved from the common slime. But she will never accept the fact that man is not exempt from the peace-keeping law of the community of life. To accept that would finish her off."

"So what are you saying? That it's hopeless?"

"Not at all. Obviously Mother Culture *must* be finished

off if you're going to survive, and that's something you can do. She has no existence outside your minds. Once you stop listening to her, she ceases to exist."

"True. But I don't think people will let that happen."

Ishmael shrugged. "Then the law will do it for them. If they refuse to live under the law, then they simply won't live. You might say that this is one of the law's basic operations: Those who threaten the stability of the community by defying the law automatically eliminate themselves."

"The Takers will never accept that."

"Acceptance has nothing to do with it. You may as well talk about a man stepping off the edge of a cliff not accepting the effects of gravity. The Takers are in the process of eliminating themselves, and when they've done so, the stability of the community will be restored and the damage you've done can begin to be repaired."

"True."

"On the other hand, I think you're being unreasonably pessimistic about this. I think a lot of people know the jig is up and are ready to hear something new. They *want* to hear something new, just like you."

"I hope you're right."

9

"I'm not quite satisfied with the way we've formulated this law," I said.

"No?"

"We refer to it as a law, but it's actually three laws. Or at any rate I described it as three laws."

"The three laws are branches. What you're looking for is the trunk, which is something like, 'No one species shall make the life of the world its own.'"

"Yes, that's what the rules of competition ensure."

"That's one expression of the law. Here's another: 'The world was not made for any one species.'"

"Yes. Then man was certainly not made to conquer and rule it."

"That's too big a leap. In Taker mythology, the world needed a ruler because the gods had made a mess of it. What they'd created was a jungle, a howling chaos, an anarchy. But was it that in fact?"

"No, everything was in good order. It was the Takers who introduced disorder into the world."

"The rule of that law was and is sufficient. Mankind was not needed to bring order to the world."

"That's right."

10

"The people of your culture cling with fanatical tenacity to the specialness of man. They want desperately to perceive a vast gulf between man and the rest of creation. This mythology of human superiority justifies their doing whatever they please with the world, just the way Hitler's mythology of Aryan superiority justified his doing whatever he pleased with Europe. But in the end this mythology is not deeply satisfying. The Takers are a profoundly lonely people. The world for them is enemy territory, and they live in it everywhere like an army of occupation, alienated and isolated by their extraordinary specialness."

"That's true. But what are you getting at?"

Instead of answering my question, Ishmael said, "Among the Leavers, crime, mental illness, suicide, and drug addiction are great rarities. How does Mother Culture account for this?"

"I'd say it's because . . . She says it's because the Leavers are just too primitive to have these things."

"In other words, crime, mental illness, suicide, and drug addiction are features of an advanced culture."

"That's right. Nobody says it that way, of course, but that's how it's understood. These things are the price of advancement."

"There's an almost opposite opinion that has had wide currency in your culture for a century or so. An opposite opinion as to why these things are rare among the Leavers."

I thought for a minute. "You mean the Noble Savage theory. I can't say I know it in any detail."

"But you have an impression of it."

"Yes."

"That's what's current in your culture—not the theory in detail but an impression of it."

"True. It's the idea that people living close to nature tend to be noble. It's seeing all those sunsets and thunderstorms that does it. I don't know. You can't watch a sunset and then go off and set fire to your neighbor's tepee. Living close to nature is wonderful for your mental health."

"I trust you know I'm not saying anything like this."

"Yes. But what *are* you saying?"

"We've had a look at the story the Takers have been enacting here for the past ten thousand years. The Leavers too are enacting a story. Not a story told but a story enacted."

"What do you mean by that?"

"If you go among the various peoples of your culture—if you go to China and Japan and Russia and England and India—each people will give you a completely different account of themselves, but they are nonetheless all enacting a single basic story, which is the story of the Takers."

"Okay."

"The same is true of the Leavers. The Bushmen of Africa, the Alawa of Australia, the Kreen-Akrore of Brazil, and the Navajo of the United States would each give you a different account of themselves, but they too are all enacting one basic story, which is the story of the Leavers."

"I see what you're getting at. It isn't the tale you tell that counts, it's the way you actually live."

"That's correct. The story the Takers have been enacting here for the past ten thousand years is not only disastrous for mankind and for the world, it's fundamentally unhealthy and unsatisfying. It's a megalomaniac's fantasy, and enacting it has given the Takers a culture riddled with greed, cruelty, mental illness, crime, and drug addiction."

"Yes, that seems to be so."

"The story the Leavers have been enacting here for the past three million years isn't a story of conquest and rule. Enacting it doesn't give them power. Enacting it gives them lives that are satisfying and meaningful to them. This is what you'll find if you go among them. They're not seething with discontent and rebellion, not incessantly wrangling over what should be allowed and what forbidden, not forever accusing each other of not living the right way, not living in terror of each other, not going crazy because their lives seem empty and pointless, not having to stupefy themselves with drugs to get through the days, not inventing a new religion every week to give them something to hold on to, not forever searching for something to do or something to believe in that will make their lives worth living. And—I repeat—this is not because they live close to nature or have no formal government or because they're innately noble. This is simply because they're enacting a story that works well for people—a story that worked well for three million years and that still works well where the Takers haven't yet managed to stamp it out."

"Okay. That sounds terrific. When do we get to that story?"

"Tomorrow. At least we'll begin tomorrow."

"Good," I said. "But before we quit today, I have a question."

"Proceed."

"Why *Mother* Culture? I personally have no difficulty with it, but I can imagine that some women would, on the grounds that you seem to be singling out a figure of *specifically* female gender to serve as a cultural villain."

Ishmael grunted. "I don't consider her a *villain* in any sense whatever, but I understand what you're getting at. Here is my answer: Culture is a mother everywhere and at every time, because culure is inherently a nurturer—the nurturer of human societies and life-styles. Among Leaver peoples, Mother Culture explains and preserves a life-style that is healthy and self-sustaining. Among Taker peoples she explains and preserves a life-style that has proven to be unhealthy and self-destructive."

"Okay. So?"

"So what's your question? If culture is a mother among the Alawa of Australia and the Bushmen of Africa and the Kayapo of Brazil, then why wouldn't she be a mother among the Takers?"

"I don't know." He glared at me, and I shrugged. "I asked, that's all."

NINE

1

When I arrived the next day, I found that a new plan was in effect: Ishmael was no longer on the other side of the glass, he was on my side of it, sprawled on some cushions a few feet from my chair. I hadn't realized how important that sheet of glass had become to our relationship: to be honest, I felt a flutter of alarm in my stomach. His nearness and enormousness disconcerted me, but without hesitating for more than a fraction of a second, I took my seat and gave him my usual nod of greeting. He nodded back, but I thought I glimpsed a look of wary speculation in his eyes, as if my proximity troubled him as much as his troubled me.

"Before we go on," Ishmael said after a few moments, "I want to clear up a misconception." He held up a pad of drawing paper with a diagram on it.

"Not a particularly difficult visualization. It represents the story line of the Leavers," he said.

"Yes, I see."

He added something and held it up again.

"This offshoot, beginning at about 8000 B.C., represents the story line of the Takers."

"Right."

"And what event does this represent?" he asked, touching the point of his pencil to the dot labeled 8000 B.C.

"The agricultural revolution."

"Did this event occur at a point in time or over a period of time?"

"I assume over a period of time."

"Then this dot at 8000 B.C. represents what?"

"The beginning of the revolution."

"Where shall I put the dot to show when it ended?"

"Ah," I said witlessly. "I don't really know. It must have lasted a couple thousand years."

"What event marked the end of the revolution?"

"Again, I don't know. I don't know that any particular event *would* have marked it."

"No popping champagne corks?"

"I don't know."

"Think."

I thought, and after a while said, "Okay. It's strange that this isn't taught. I remember being taught about the agricultural revolution, but I don't remember this."

"Go on."

"It didn't end. It just spread. It's been spreading ever since it began back there ten thousand years ago. It spread across this continent during the eighteenth and nineteenth centuries. It's still spreading across parts of New Zealand and Africa and South America today."

"Of course. So you see that your agricultural revolution is not an event like the Trojan War, isolated in the distant past and without direct relevance to your lives today. The work begun by those neolithic farmers in the Near East has been carried forward from one generation to the next without a single break, right into the present moment. It's the foundation of your vast civilization today in exactly the same way that it was the foundation of the very first farming village."

"Yes, I see that."

"This should help you understand why the story you tell your children about the meaning of the world, about divine intentions in the world, and about the destiny of man is of such profound importance to the people of your culture. It's the manifesto of the revolution on which your culture is based. It's the repository of all your revolutionary doctrine and the definitive expression of your revolutionary spirit. It explains why the revolution was necessary and why it must be carried forward at any cost whatever."

"Yes," I said. "That's quite a thought."

2

"About two thousand years ago," Ishmael went on, "an event of exquisite irony occurred within your culture. The Takers—or at least a very large segment of them—adopted as their own a story that seemed to them pregnant with meaning and mystery. It came to them from a Taker people of the Near East who had been telling it to their own children for countless generations—for so many generations that it had become a mystery even to them. Do you know why?"

"Why it had become a mystery? No."

"It had become a mystery because those who first told the story—their ancient ancestors—were not Takers but Leavers."

I sat there for a while blinking at him. Then I asked him if he'd mind running that past me again.

"About two thousand years ago, the Takers adopted as their own a story that had originated among Leavers many centuries before."

"Okay. What's the irony in that?"

"The irony is that it was a story that had once been told among Leavers about the origins of the Takers."

"So?"

"The Takers adopted *as their own* a Leaver story about their origins."

"I'm afraid I just don't get it."

"What sort of story would a Leaver people tell about the appearance of the Takers in the world?"

"God, I have no idea."

Ishmael peered at me owlishly. "You seem to have forgotten to take your brainy pill this morning. Never mind, I'll tell you a story of my own, and then you'll see it."

"Okay."

Ishmael shifted his mountainous bulk into a new position on his pillows, and involuntarily I closed my eyes, thinking, *If a stranger were to open the door and walk in at this moment, what on earth would he think?*

3

"There is a very special knowledge you must have if you're going to rule the world," Ishmael said. "I'm sure you realize that."

"Frankly, I've never thought about it."

"The Takers possess this knowledge, of course—at least they imagine they do—and they're very, very proud of it. This is the most fundamental knowledge of all, and it's absolutely indispensable to those who would rule the world. And what do you suppose the Takers find when they go among the Leavers?"

"I don't know what you mean."

"They find that the Leavers do not have this knowledge. Isn't that remarkable?"

"I don't know."

"Consider it. The Takers have a knowledge that enables them to rule the world, and the Leavers lack it. This is what the missionaries found wherever they went among the Leavers. They were quite astonished themselves, because they had the impression that this knowledge was virtually self-evident."

"I don't even know what knowledge you're talking about."

"It's the knowledge that's needed to rule the world."

"Okay, but specifically what knowledge *is* that?"

"You'll learn that from the story. What I'm looking at right now is *who has this knowledge*. I've told you that the Takers have it, and that makes sense, doesn't it? The Takers are the rulers of the world, aren't they?"

"Yes."

"And the Leavers don't have it, and that too makes sense, doesn't it?"

"I guess so."

"Now tell me this: Who else would have this knowledge, besides the Takers?"

"I have no idea."

"Think mythologically."

"Okay. . . . The gods would have it."

"Of course. And that's what my story is about: How the gods acquired the knowledge they needed to rule the world."

4

One day (Ishmael began) the gods were considering the administration of the world in the ordinary way, and one of them said, "Here's a spot I've been thinking about for a while—a wide, pleasant savannah. Let's send a great multitude of locusts into this land. Then the fire of life will grow prodigiously in them and in the birds and lizards that will feed on them, and that will be very fine."

The others thought about this for a while, then one said, "It's certainly true that, if we send the locusts into this land, the fire of life will blaze in them and in the creatures that feed on them—but at the expense of all the other creatures that live there." The others asked him what his point was, and he went on. "Surely it would be a great crime to deprive all these other creatures of the fire of life so that the locusts and the birds and the lizards can flourish for a time. For the locusts will strip the land bare, and the deer and the gazelles and the goats and the rabbits will go hungry and die. And with the disappearance of the game, the lions and the wolves and the foxes will soon be dying too. Won't they curse us then and call us criminals for favoring the locusts and the birds and the lizards over them?"

Now the gods had to scratch their heads over this, because they'd never looked at matters in this particular light before. But finally one of them said, "I don't see that this presents any great problem. We simply won't do it. We won't raise a multitude of locusts to send into this land, then things will go on as before, and no one will have any reason to curse us."

Most of the gods thought this made sense, but one of them disagreed. "Surely this would be as great a crime as the other," he said. "For don't the locusts and the birds and the lizards live in our hands as well as the rest? Is it never to be their time to flourish greatly, as others do?"

While the gods were debating this point, a fox came out to hunt, and they said, "Let's send the fox a quail for its life." But these words were hardly spoken when one of them said, "Surely it would be a crime to let the fox live at the quail's expense. The quail has its life that we gave it and lives in our hands. It would be infamous to send it into the jaws of the fox!"

Then another said, "Look here! The quail is stalking a grasshopper! If we don't give the quail to the fox, then the quail will eat the grasshopper. Doesn't the grasshopper have its life that we gave it and doesn't it live in our hands as truly as the quail? Surely it would be a crime *not* to give the quail to the fox, so that the grasshopper may live."

Well, as you can imagine, the gods groaned heavily over this and didn't know what to do. And while they were wrangling over it, spring came, and the snow waters of the mountains began to swell the streams, and one of them said, "Surely it would be a crime to let these waters flood the land, for countless creatures are bound to be carried off to their deaths." But then another said, "Surely it would be a crime *not* to let these waters flood the land, for without them the ponds and marshes will dry up, and all the creatures that live in them will die." And once more the gods were thrown into confusion.

Finally one of them had what seemed to be a new thought. "It's clear that any action we take will be good for some and evil for others, so let's take no action at all. Then none of the creatures that live in our hands can call us criminals."

"Nonsense," another snapped. "If we take no action at all, this will also be good for some and evil for others, won't it? The creatures that live in our hands will say, 'Look, we suffer, and the gods do nothing!'"

And while the gods bickered among themselves, the locusts swarmed over the savannah, and the locusts and the birds and the lizards praised the gods while the game and the predators died cursing the gods. And because the gods had taken no action in the matter, the quail lived, and the fox went hungry to its hole cursing the gods. And because the quail lived, it ate the grasshopper, and the grasshopper died cursing the gods. And because in the end the gods decided to stem the flood of spring waters, the ponds and the marshes dried up, and all the thousands of creatures that lived in them died cursing the gods.

And hearing all these curses, the gods groaned. "We've made the garden a place of terror, and all that live in it hate us as tyrants and criminals. And they're right to do this, because by action or inaction we send them good one day and evil the next without knowing what we should do. The savannah stripped by the locusts rings with curses, and we have no answer to make. The fox and the grasshopper curse us because we let the quail live, and we have no answer to make. Surely the whole world must curse the day we made it, for we are criminals who send good and evil by turns, knowing even as we do it that we don't know what ought to be done."

Well, the gods were sinking right into the slough of despond when one of them looked up and said, "Say, didn't we make for the garden a certain tree whose fruit is the knowledge of good and evil?"

"Yes," cried the others. "Let's find that tree and eat of it and see what this knowledge is." And when the gods had found this tree and had tasted its fruit, their eyes were opened, and they said, "Now indeed we have the knowledge we need to tend the garden without becoming criminals and without earning the curses of all who live in our hands."

And as they were talking in this way, a lion went out to hunt, and the gods said to themselves, "Today is the lion's day to go hungry, and the deer it would have taken may live another day." And so the lion missed its kill, and as it was returning hungry to its den it began to curse the gods. But they said, "Be at peace, for we know how to rule the world, and today is your day to go hungry." And the lion was at peace.

And the next day the lion went out to hunt, and the gods sent it the deer they had spared the day before. And as the deer felt the lion's jaws on its neck, it began to curse the gods. But they said, "Be at peace, for we know how to rule the world, and today is your day to die just as yesterday was your day to live." And the deer was at peace.

Then the gods said to themselves, "Certainly the knowledge of good and evil is a powerful knowledge, for it enables us to rule the world without becoming criminals. If we had yesterday sent the lion away hungry without this knowledge, then indeed it would have been a crime. And if we had today sent the deer into the lion's jaws without this knowledge, then indeed this too would have been a crime. But with this knowledge we have done both of these things, one seemingly opposed to the other, and have committed no crime."

Now it happened that one of the gods was away on an errand when the others were eating at the tree of knowledge, and when he returned and heard what the gods had done in the matter of the lion and the deer, he said, "In doing these two things you have surely committed a crime in one instance or the other, for these two things are opposed, and one must have been right to do and the other wrong. If it was good for the lion to go hungry on the first day, then it was evil to send it the deer on the second. Or if it was good to send it the deer on the second day, then it was evil to send it away hungry on the first."

The others nodded and said, "Yes, this is just the way we would have reasoned before we ate of this tree of knowledge."

"What knowledge is this?" the god asked, noticing the tree for the first time.

"Taste its fruit," they told him. "Then you'll know exactly what knowledge it is."

So the god tasted, and his eyes were opened. "Yes, I see," he said. "This is indeed the proper knowledge of the gods: *the knowledge of who shall live and who shall die.*"

5

"Any questions so far?" Ishmael asked.

I jumped, startled by this break in the narrative. "No. This is fascinating."

Ishmael went on.

6

When the gods saw that Adam was awakening, they said to themselves, "Now here is a creature so like us that he might almost be one of our company. What span of life and what destiny shall we fashion for him?"

One of them said, "He is so fair, let's give him life for the lifetime of this planet. In the days of his childhood let's care for him as we care for all others in the garden, so that he learns the sweetness of living in our hands. But in adolescence he will surely begin to realize that he's capable of much more than other creatures and will become restless in our care. Shall we then lead him to the other tree in the garden, the Tree of Life?"

But another said, "To lead Adam like a child to the Tree of Life before he had even begun to seek it for himself would deprive him of a great undertaking by which he may gain an important wisdom and prove his mettle to himself. As we would give him the care he needs as a child, let's give him the quest he needs as an adolescent. Let's make the quest for the Tree of Life the occupation of his adolescence. In this way he'll discover for himself how he may have life for the lifetime of this planet."

The others agreed with this plan, but one said, "We should take note that this might well be a long and baffling quest for Adam. Youth is impatient, and after a few thousand years of searching, he might despair of finding the Tree of Life. If this should happen, he might be tempted to eat of the Tree of the Knowledge of Good and Evil instead."

"Nonsense," the others replied. "You know very well that the fruit of this tree nourishes only the gods. It can no more nourish Adam than the grasses of the oxen. He might take it into his mouth and swallow it, but it would pass through his body without benefit. Surely you don't imagine that he might actually gain our knowledge by eating of this tree?"

"Of course not," the other replied. "The danger is not that he would gain our knowledge but rather that he might *imagine* that he'd gained it. Having tasted the fruit of this tree, he might say to himself, 'I have eaten at the gods' own tree of knowledge and therefore know as well as they how to rule the world. I may do as I will.'"

"This is absurd," said the other gods. "How could Adam ever be so foolish as to imagine he had the knowledge that enables us to govern the world and to do what we will do?

None of our creatures will ever be master of the knowledge of who shall live and who shall die. This knowledge is ours alone, and if Adam should grow in wisdom till the very eclipse of the universe, it would be as far beyond him as it is right now."

But the other was not disconcerted by this argument. "If Adam should eat of our tree," he persisted, "there's no telling how he might deceive himself. Not knowing the truth, he might say to himself, 'Whatever I can justify doing is good and whatever I cannot justify doing is evil.'"

But the others scoffed at this, saying, "This is not the knowledge of good and evil."

"Of course it's not," the other replied, "but how would Adam know this?"

The others shrugged. "Perhaps in childhood Adam might believe he was wise enough to rule the world, but what of it? Such arrogant foolishness would pass with maturity."

"Ah," said the other, "but possessed of this arrogant foolishness, would Adam *survive* into maturity? Believing himself our equal, he would be capable of anything. In his arrogance, he might look around the garden and say to himself, 'This is all wrong. Why should I have to share the fire of life with all these creatures? Look here, the lions and the wolves and the foxes take the game I would have for myself. This is evil. I will kill all these creatures, and this will be good. And look here, the rabbits and the grasshoppers and the sparrows take the fruits of the land that I would have for myself. This is evil. I will kill all these creatures, and this will be good. And look here, the gods have set a limit on my growth just as they've set a limit on the growth of all others. This is evil. I will grow without limit, taking all the fire of life that flows through this garden into myself, and that will be good.' Tell me—if this should happen, how long would Adam live before he had devoured the entire world?"

"If this should happen," the others said, "Adam would

devour the world in a single day, and at the end of that day he would devour himself."

"Just so," the other said, "unless he managed to escape from this world. Then he would devour the entire universe as he had devoured the world. But even so he would inevitably end by devouring himself, as anything must that grows without limit."

"This would indeed be a terrible end for Adam," another said. "But might he not come to the same end even without having eaten at the Tree of Knowledge of Good and Evil? Might he not be tempted by his yearning for growth to take the fire of life into his own hands even without deluding himself that this was good?"

"He might," the others agreed. "But what would be the result? He would become a criminal, an outlaw, a thief of life, and a murderer of the creatures around him. Without the delusion that what he was doing was good—and therefore to be done at any cost—he would soon weary of the outlaw's life. Indeed this is bound to happen during his quest for the Tree of Life. But if he should eat of the tree of our knowledge, then he will shrug off his weariness. He will say, 'What does it matter that I'm weary of living as a murderer of all the life around me? I know good and evil, and this way of living is good. Therefore I must live this way even though I'm weary unto death, even though I destroy the world and even myself. The gods wrote in the world a law for all to follow, but it cannot apply to me because I'm their equal. Therefore I will live outside this law and grow without limit. To be limited is evil. I will steal the fire of life from the hands of the gods and heap it up for my growth, and that will be good. I will destroy those kinds that do not serve my growth, and that will be good. I will wrest the garden from the hands of the gods and order it anew so that it serves only my growth, and that will be good. And because these things are good, they must be done at any cost. It may be that I'll destroy the garden and make a ruin of it. It may be that my progeny will teem over the earth like locusts, stripping it bare, until they drown in their own filth and hate the very sight of one another and go mad. Still they must go on, because to grow without limit is good and to accept the limits of the law is evil. And if any say, "Let's put off the burdens of the criminal life and live in the hands of the gods once again," I will kill them, for what they say is evil. And if any say, "Let's turn aside from our misery and search for that other tree," I will kill them, for what they say is evil. And when at last all the garden has been subjugated to my use and all kinds that do not serve my growth have been cast aside and all the fire of life in the world flows through my progeny, still I must grow. And to the people of this land I will say, "Grow, for this is good," and they will grow. And to the people of the next land I will say, "Grow, for this is good," and they will grow. And when they can grow no more, the people of this land will fall upon the people of the next to murder them, so that they may grow still more. And if the groans of my progeny fill the air throughout the world, I will say to them, "Your sufferings must be borne, for you suffer in the cause of good. See how great we have become! Wielding the knowledge of good and evil, we have made ourselves the masters of the world, and the gods have no power over us. Though your groans fill the air, isn't it sweeter to live in our own hands than in the hands of the gods?"'"

And when the gods heard all this, they saw that, of all the trees in the garden, only the Tree of the Knowledge of Good and Evil could destroy Adam. And so they said to him, "You may eat of every tree in the garden save the Tree of the Knowledge of Good and Evil, for on the day you eat of that tree you will certainly die."

7

I sat there dazed for a while, then I recalled seeing a bible in Ishmael's odd collection of books. In fact, there were three. I fetched them and after a few minutes of study looked up and said, "None of these has any comment to make on why this tree should have been forbidden to Adam."

"Were you expecting them to?"

"Well . . . yes."

"The Takers write the notes, and this story has always been an impenetrable mystery to them. They've never been able to figure out why the knowledge of good and evil should have been forbidden to man. Don't you see why?"

"No."

"Because, to the Takers, this knowledge is the very best knowledge of all—the most beneficial for man to have. This being so, why would the gods forbid it to him?"

"True."

"The knowledge of good and evil is fundamentally the knowledge the rulers of the world must exercise, because every single thing they do is good for some but evil for others. This is what ruling is all about, isn't it?"

"Yes."

"And man was born to rule the world, wasn't he?"

"Yes. According to Taker mythology."

"Then why would the gods withhold the very knowledge man needs to fulfill his destiny? From the Taker point of view, it makes no sense at all."

"True."

"The disaster occurred when, ten thousand years ago, the people of your culture said, 'We're as wise as the gods and can rule the world as well as they.' When they took *into their own hands* the power of life and death over the world, their doom was assured."

"Yes. Because they are not in fact as wise as the gods."

"The gods ruled the world for billions of years, and it was doing just fine. After just a few thousand years of human rule, the world is at the point of death."

"True. But the Takers will never give it up."

Ishmael shrugged. "Then they'll die. As predicted. The authors of this story knew what they were talking about."

8

"And you're saying this story was written from a Leaver point of view?"

"That's right. If it had been written from the Taker point of view, the knowledge of good and evil wouldn't have been forbidden to Adam, it would have been *thrust* upon him. The gods would have hung around saying, 'Come on, Man, can't you see that you're nothing without this knowledge? Stop living off our bounty like a lion or a wombat. Here, have some of this fruit and you'll instantly realize that you're naked—as naked as any lion or wombat: naked to the world, powerless. Come on, have some of this fruit and become one of us. Then, lucky you, you can leave this garden and begin living by the sweat of your brow, the way humans are supposed to live.' And if people of your cultural persuasion had authored it, this event wouldn't be called the Fall, it would be called the Ascent—or as you put it earlier, the Liberation."

"Very true. . . . But I'm not quite sure how this fits in with everything else."

"We are furthering your understanding of *how things came to be this way*."

"I don't get it."

"A minute ago, you told me that the Takers will never

give up their tyranny over the world, no matter how bad things get. How did they get to be this way?"

I goggled at him.

"They got to be this way because they've always believed that what they were doing was *right*—and therefore to be done at any cost whatever. They've always believed that, like the gods, they know what is right to do and what is wrong to do, and what they're doing is *right*. Do you see how they've demonstrated what I'm saying?"

"Not offhand."

"They've demonstrated it by forcing everyone in the world to do what *they* do, to live the way *they* live. Everyone had to be forced to live like the Takers, because the Takers had the one *right* way."

"Yes, I can see that."

"Many peoples among the Leavers practiced agriculture, but they were never obsessed by the delusion that what they were doing was *right*, that everyone in the entire world had to practice agriculture, that every last square yard of the planet had to be devoted to it. They didn't say to the people around them, 'You may no longer live by hunting and gathering. This is wrong. This is evil, and we forbid it. Put your land under cultivation or we'll wipe you out.' What they said was, 'You want to be hunter-gatherers? That's fine with us. That's great. We want to be agriculturalists. You be hunter-gatherers and we'll be agriculturalists. We don't pretend to know which way is *right*. We just know which way we *prefer*.'"

"Yes, I see."

"And if they got tired of being agriculturalists, if they found they didn't like where it was leading them in their particular adaptation, they were *able* to give it up. They didn't say to themselves, 'Well, we've got to keep going at this even if it kills us, because this is the *right* way to live.' For example, there was once a people who constructed a vast network of irrigation canals in order to farm the deserts of what is now southeastern Arizona. They maintained these canals for three thousand years and built a fairly advanced civilization, but in the end they were free to say, 'This is a toilsome and unsatisfying way to live, so to hell with it.' They simply walked away from the whole thing and put it so totally out of mind that we don't even know what they called themselves. The only name we have for them is one the Pima Indians gave them: Hohokam—those who vanished.

"But it's not going to be this easy for the Takers. It's going to be hard as hell for them to give it up, because what they're doing is *right,* and they have to go on doing it even if it means destroying the world and mankind with it."

"Yes, that's the way it seems."

"Giving it up would mean . . . what?"

"Giving it up would mean . . . It would mean that all along they'd been *wrong.* It would mean that they'd *never* known how to rule the world. It would mean . . . relinquishing their pretensions to godhood."

"It would mean spitting out the fruit of that tree and giving the rule of the world back to the gods."

"Yes."

9

Ishmael nodded to the stack of bibles at my feet. "According to the authors of that story, the people living between the Tigris and Euphrates rivers had eaten at the gods' own tree of knowledge. Where do you suppose they got that idea?"

"What do you mean?"

"Whatever gave the authors of this story the idea that the people living in the Fertile Crescent had eaten at the gods' tree of knowledge? Do you suppose they saw it with their own eyes? Do you suppose they were there when your agricultural revolution began?"

"I suppose that's a possibility."

"Think. If they'd been there to see it with their own eyes, who would they have been?"

"Oh . . . right. They would have been the people of the Fall. They would have been the Takers."

"And if they'd been Takers, they would have told the story a different way."

"Yes."

"So the authors of this story were not there to see it with their own eyes. How then did they know it had happened? How did they know that the Takers had usurped the role of the gods in the world?"

"Lord," I said.

"Who *were* the authors of this story?"

"Well . . . the Hebrews?"

Ishmael shook his head. "Among the people known as the Hebrews, this was already an ancient story—and a mysterious story. The Hebrews stepped into history as Takers—and wanted nothing more than to be like their Taker neighbors. Indeed, that's why their prophets were always bawling them out."

"True."

"So, though they preserved the story, they no longer fully understood it. To find the people who understood it, we have to find its authors. And who were they?"

"Well . . . they were the ancestors of the Hebrews."

"But who were *they*?"

"I'm afraid I have no idea."

Ishmael grunted. "Look, I can't forbid you to say, 'I have no idea,' but I do insist that you spend a few seconds *thinking* before you say it."

I spent a few seconds at it, just to be polite, then I said, "I'm sorry. My grasp of ancient history is frankly negligible."

"The ancient ancestors of the Hebrews were the Semites."

"Oh."

"You knew that, didn't you?"

"Yes, I guess so. I just . . ."

"You just weren't thinking."

"Right."

Ishmael bestirred himself, and to be perfectly honest, my stomach clenched as the half ton of him brushed past my chair. If you don't know how gorillas make their way from place to place on the ground, you can visit the zoo or rent a *National Geographic* videotape; no words of mine will make you see it.

Ishmael lumbered or shambled or shuffled over to the bookcase and returned with an historical atlas, which he handed to me open to a map of Europe and the Near East in 8500 B.C. A blade like a hand sickle very nearly cut the Arabian peninsula away from the rest. The words *Incipient Agriculture* made it clear that the sickle blade enclosed the Fertile Crescent. A handful of dots indicated sites where early farming implements had been found.

"This map, I feel, gives a false impression," Ishmael said, "though it was not an intended impression. It gives the impression that the agricultural revolution took place in an empty world. This is why I prefer my own map." He opened his pad and showed it to me.

"As you see, this shows the situation five hundred years later. The agricultural revolution is well under way. The area in which farming is taking place is indicated by these hen-scratches." Using a pencil as a pointer, he indicated the area between the Tigris and the Euphrates. "This, of course, is the land between the rivers, the birthplace of the Takers. And what do you suppose all these dots represent?"

"Leaver peoples?"

"Exactly. They're not designed as a statement about population density. Nor are they intended to indicate that

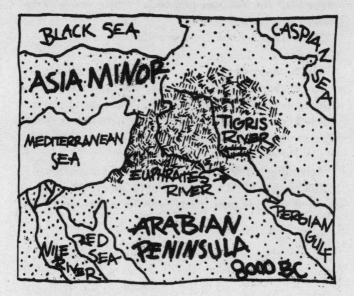

every available stretch of land was inhabited by some Leaver people. What they indicate is that this was far from being an empty world. Do you see what I'm showing you?"

"Well, I think so. The land of the Fall lay within the Fertile Crescent and was surrounded by nonagriculturalists."

"Yes, but I'm also pointing out that at this time, at the beginning of your agricultural revolution, these early Takers, the founders of your culture, were unknown, isolated, unimportant. The next map in that historical atlas is four thousand years later. What would you expect to see on it?"

"I'd expect to see that the Takers have expanded."

He nodded, indicating that I should turn the page. Here a printed oval, labeled *Chalcolithic Cultures*, with Mesopotamia at its center, enclosed the whole of Asia Minor and all the land to the north and east as far as the Caspian Sea and the Persian Gulf. The oval extended southward as far as the entrance to the Arabian peninsula, which was a cross-hatched area labeled *Semites*.

"Now," Ishmael said, "we have some witnesses."

"How so?"

"The Semites were not eyewitnesses to the events described in chapter three of Genesis." He drew a small oval in the center of the Fertile Crescent. "Those events, cumulatively known as the Fall, took place here, hundreds of miles north of the Semites, among an entirely different people. Do you see who they were?"

"According to the map, they were the Caucasians."

"But now, in 4500 B.C., the Semites are eyewitnesses to an event in their own front yard: the expansion of the Takers."

"Yes, I see."

"In four thousand years the agricultural revolution that began in the land between the rivers had spread across Asia Minor to the west and to the mountains in the north and east. And to the south it seems to have been blocked by what?"

"By the Semites, apparently."

"Why? Why were the Semites blocking it?"

"I don't know."

"What were the Semites? Were they agriculturalists?"

"No. The map makes it clear that they weren't a part of what was going on among the Takers. So I assume they were Leavers."

"Leavers, yes, but no longer hunter-gatherers. They had evolved another adaptation that was to be traditional for Semitic peoples."

"Oh. They were pastoralists."

"Of course. Herders." He indicated the border between the Takers' Chalcolithic Culture and the Semites. "So what was happening here?"

"I don't know."

Ishmael nodded toward the bibles at my feet. "Read the story of Cain and Abel in Genesis and then you'll know."

I picked up the one on top and turned to chapter four. A couple minutes later, I muttered, "Good lord."

10

After reading the story in all three versions, I looked up and said, "What was happening along that border was that Cain was killing Abel. The tillers of the soil were watering their fields with the blood of Semitic herders."

"Of course. What was happening there was what has always happened along the borders of Taker expansion: The Leavers were being killed off so that more land could be put under cultivation." Ishmael picked up his pad and opened it to his own map of this period. "As you see, the hen-scratches of the agriculturalists have swarmed over the entire area—except for the territory occupied by the Semites. Here at the border that separates tillers of the soil from Semitic herders, Cain and Abel confront each other."

I studied the map for a few moments and then shook my head. "And biblical scholars don't understand this?"

"I cannot say, of course, that not a single scholar has ever understood this. But most read the story as if it were set in an historical never-never land, like one of Aesop's fables. It would scarcely occur to them to understand it as a piece of Semitic war propaganda."

"That's what it is, all right. I know it's always been a mystery as to why God accepted Abel and his offering and rejected Cain and his offering. This explains it. With this story, the Semites were telling their children, 'God is on our side. He loves us herders but hates those murderous tillers of the soil from the north.'"

"That's right. If you read it as a story that originated among your own cultural ancestors, it's incomprehensible.

It only begins to make sense when you realize that it originated among the *enemies* of your cultural ancestors."

"Yes." I sat there blinking for a few moments, then looked at Ishmael's map again. "If the tillers of the soil from the north were Caucasians," I said, "then the mark of Cain is *this*." I pointed to my own fair or maggot-colored face.

"It could be. Obviously we'll never know for sure what the authors of the story had in mind."

"But it makes *sense* this way," I insisted. "The mark was given to Cain as a warning to others: 'Leave this man alone. This is a dangerous man, one who exacts a sevenfold vengeance.' Certainly a lot of people all over the world have learned that it doesn't pay to mess with people with white faces."

Ishmael shrugged, unconvinced or perhaps just uninterested.

11

"In the previous map, I went to the trouble of laying down hundreds of dots to represent Leaver peoples living in the Mideast when your agricultural revolution began. What do you suppose happened to these peoples between the time of that map and the time of this map?"

"I would have to say that either they were overrun and assimilated or they took up agriculture in imitation of the Takers."

Ishmael nodded. "Doubtless many of these peoples had their own tales to tell of this revolution, their own ways of explaining how these people from the Fertile Crescent came to be the way they were, but only one of these tales survived—the one told by the Semites to their children about the Fall of Adam and the slaughter of Abel by his brother Cain. It survived because the Takers never managed to overrun the Semites, and the Semites refused to take up the agricultural life. Even their eventual Taker descendants, the Hebrews, who preserved the story without fully understanding it, couldn't work up any enthusiasm for the peasant life-style. And this is how it happened that, with the spread of Christianity and of the Old Testament, the Takers came to adopt as their own a story an enemy once told to denounce them."

12

"So we come again to this question: Where did the Semites get the idea that the people of the Fertile Crescent had eaten at the gods' own tree of knowledge?"

"Ah," I said. "I would say it was a sort of reconstruction. They looked at the people they were fighting and said, 'My God, how did they *get* this way?'"

"And what was their answer?"

"Well . . . 'What's *wrong* with these people? What's wrong with our brothers from the north? Why are they doing this to us? They act like . . .' Let me think about this for a bit."

"Take your time."

"Okay," I said a few minutes later. "Here's how it would look to the Semites, I think. 'What's going on here is something wholly new. These aren't raiding parties. These aren't people drawing a line and baring their teeth at us to make sure we know they're there. These guys are saying . . . Our brothers from the north are saying that we've got to die. They're saying Abel has to be wiped out. They're saying we're not to be allowed to live. Now that's something new, and we don't get it. Why can't they live up there and be farmers and let us live down here and be herders? Why do they have to murder us?

"'Something really weird must have happened up there to turn these people into murderers. What could it have been? Wait a second . . . Look at the way these people live. Nobody has ever lived this way before. They're not just saying that *we* have to die. They're saying that *everything* has to die. They're not just killing us, they're killing *everything*. They're saying, "Okay, lions, you're dead. We've had it with you. You're out of here." They're saying, "Okay, wolves, we've had it with you too. You're out of here." They're saying . . . "Nobody eats but us. All this food belongs to us and no one else can have any without our permission." They're saying, "What we want to live lives and what we want to die dies."

"'That's it! They're acting as if they were the gods themselves. They're acting as if they eat at the gods' own tree of wisdom, as though they were as wise as the gods and could send life and death wherever they please. Yes, that's it. That's what must have happened up there. These people found the gods' own tree of wisdom and stole some of its fruit.

"'Aha! Right! These are an accursed people! You can see that right off the bat. When the gods found out what they'd done, they said, "Okay, you wretched people, that's it for you! We're not taking care of you anymore. You're out. We banish you from the garden. From now on, instead of living on our bounty, you can wrest your food from the ground by the sweat of your brows." And that's how these accursed tillers of the soil came to be hunting us down and watering their fields with our blood.'"

When I finished, I saw that Ishmael was putting his hands together in mute applause.

I replied with a smirk and a modest nod.

13

"One of the clearest indications that these two stories were not authored by your cultural ancestors is the fact that agriculture is not portrayed as a desirable choice, freely made, but rather as a curse. It was literally inconceivable to the authors of these stories that anyone would *prefer* to live by the sweat of his brow. So the question they asked themselves was not, 'Why did these people adopt this toilsome life-style?' It was, 'What terrible misdeed did these people commit to deserve such a punishment? What have they done to make the gods withhold from them the bounty that enables the rest of us to live a carefree life?'"

"Yes, that's obvious now. In our own cultural history, the adoption of agriculture was a prelude to ascent. In these stories, agriculture is the lot of the fallen."

14

"I have a question," I said. "Why did they describe Cain as Adam's firstborn and Abel as Adam's secondborn?"

Ishmael nodded. "The significance is mythological rather than chronological. I mean that you'll find this motif in folktales everywhere: When you have a father with two sons, one worthy and one unworthy, the unworthy son is almost always the cherished firstborn, while the worthy son is the secondborn—which is to say, the underdog in the story."

"Okay. But why would they think of themselves as descendants of Adam at all?"

"You mustn't confuse metaphorical thinking with biological thinking. The Semites didn't think of Adam as their biological ancestor."

"How do you know that?"

Ishmael thought for a moment. "Do you know what *Adam* means in Hebrew? We can't know the name the Semites gave him, but presumably it had the same meaning."

"It means *man*."

"Of course. The human race. Do you suppose the Semites thought that the human race was their biological ancestor?"

"No, of course not."

"I agree. The relationships in the story have to be understood metaphorically, not biologically. As they perceived it, the Fall divided the race of man into two—into bad guys and good guys, into tillers of the soil and herders, the former bent on murdering the latter."

"Okay," I said.

15

"But I'm afraid I have another question."

"There's no need to apologize for it. That's what you're here for."

"Okay. My question is, how does Eve figure in all this?"

"Her name means what?"

"According to the notes, it means *Life*."

"Not *Woman*?"

"No, not according to the notes."

"With this name, the authors of the story have made it clear that Adam's temptation wasn't sex or lust or uxoriousness. Adam was tempted by *Life*."

"I don't get it."

"Consider: A hundred men and one woman does not spell a hundred babies, but one man and a hundred women does."

"So?"

"I'm pointing out that, in terms of population expansion, men and women have markedly different roles. They're by no means equal in this regard."

"Okay. But I still don't get it."

"I'm trying to put you in the frame of mind of a nonagricultural people, a people for whom population control is always a critical problem. Let me put it baldly: A band of herders that consists of fifty men and one woman is in no danger of experiencing a population explosion, but a band that consists of one man and fifty women is in big trouble. People being people, that band of fifty-one herders is going to be a band of one hundred in no time at all."

"True. But I'm afraid I still don't see how this relates to the story in Genesis."

"Be patient. Let's go back to the authors of this story, a herding people being pushed into the desert by agriculturalists from the north. Why were their brothers from the north pushing?"

"They wanted to put the herder's land under cultivation."

"Yes, but why?"

"Ah, I see. They were increasing food production to support an expanded population."

"Of course. Now you're ready to do some more reconstruction. You can see that these tillers of the soil have no sense of restraint when it comes to expansion. They don't control their population; when there isn't enough food to go around, they just put some more land under cultivation."

"True."

"So: Whom did these people say yes to?"

"Mm. Yes, I think I see it. As in a glass, darkly."

"Think of it this way: The Semites, like most nonagricultural peoples, had to be wary of becoming overbalanced between the sexes. Having too many men didn't threaten the stability of their population, but having too many women definitely did. You see that?"

"Yes."

"But what the Semites observed in their brothers from the north was that it didn't matter to them. If their population got out of hand, they didn't worry, they just put more land under cultivation."

"Yes, I see that."

"Or try it this way: Adam and Eve spent three million years in the garden, living on the bounty of the gods, and their growth was very modest; in the Leaver life-style this is the way it *has* to be. Like Leavers everywhere, they had no need to exercise the gods' prerogative of deciding who shall live and who shall die. But when Eve presented Adam with this knowledge, he said, 'Yes, I see; with this, we no longer have to depend on the bounty of the gods. With the matter of who shall live and who shall die in our own hands, we can create a bounty that will exist for us alone, and this means I can say yes to Life, and grow without limit.' What you should understand is that saying yes to Life and accepting the knowledge of good and evil are merely different aspects of a single act, and this is the way the story is told in Genesis."

"Yes. It's subtle, but I think I see it. When Adam accepted the fruit of that tree, he succumbed to the temptation to live without limit—and so the person who offered him that fruit is named *Life*."

Ishmael nodded. "Whenever a Taker couple talk about how wonderful it would be to have a big family, they're reenacting this scene beside the Tree of the Knowledge of Good and Evil. They're saying to themselves, 'Of course it's our right to apportion life on this planet as we please. Why stop at four kids or six? We can have fifteen if we like. All we have to do is plow under another few hundred acres of rain forest—and who cares if a dozen other species disappear as a result?'"

16

There was still something that didn't quite fit together, but I couldn't figure out how to articulate it.

Ishmael told me to take my time.

After I'd sweated over it for a few minutes, he said, "Don't expect to be able to work it all out in terms of our present knowledge of the world. The Semites at this time were completely isolated on the Arabian peninsula, cut off in all directions either by the sea or by the people of Cain. For all they knew, they and their brothers to the north were literally the whole race of man, the only people on earth. Certainly that's the way they saw the story. They couldn't possibly have known that it was only in that little corner of the world that Adam had eaten at the gods' tree, couldn't possibly have known that the Fertile Crescent was only one of many places where agriculture had begun, couldn't pos-

sibly have known that there were still people all over the
world living the way Adam had lived before the Fall."

"True," I said. "I was trying to make it fit with all the
information we have, and that obviously won't work."

17

        "I think it's safe to say that the story of
Adam's Fall is by far the best-known story in the world."

"At least in the West," I said.

"Oh, it's well known in the East as well, having been
carried into every corner of the world by Christian missionaries. It has a powerful attraction for Takers everywhere."

"Yes."

"Why is that so?"

"I guess because it purports to explain what went wrong
here."

"What *did* go wrong? How do people understand the
story?"

"Adam, the first man, ate the fruit of the forbidden tree."

"And what is that understood to mean?"

"Frankly, I don't know. I've never heard an explanation
that made any sense."

"And the knowledge of good and evil?"

"Again, I've never heard an explanation that made any
sense. I think the way most people understand it, the gods
wanted to test Adam's obedience by forbidding him something, and it didn't much matter what it was. And that's what
the Fall essentially was—an act of disobedience."

"Nothing really to do with the knowledge of good and
evil."

"No. But then I suppose there are people who think that
the knowledge of good and evil is just a symbol of . . . I
don't know exactly what. They think of the Fall as a fall from
innocence."

"Innocence in this context presumably being a synonym for blissful ignorance."

"Yes . . . It's something like this: Man was innocent until he discovered the difference between good and evil. When he was no longer innocent of that knowledge, he became a fallen creature."

"I'm afraid that means nothing at all to me."

"To me either, actually."

"All the same, if you read it from another point of view, the story does explain exactly what went wrong here, doesn't it?"

"Yes."

"But the people of your culture have never been able to understand the explanation, because they've always assumed that it was formulated by people just like them—people who took it for granted that the world was made for man and man was made to conquer and rule it, people for whom the sweetest knowledge in the world is the knowledge of good and evil, people who consider tilling the soil the only noble and human way to live. Reading the story as if it had been authored by someone with their own point of view, they didn't stand a chance of understanding it."

"That's right."

"But when it's read another way, the explanation makes perfectly good sense: Man can never have the wisdom the gods use to rule the world, and if he tries to preempt that wisdom, the result won't be enlightenment, it will be death."

"Yes," I said, "I have no doubt about that—that's what the story means. Adam wasn't the progenitor of our race, he was the progenitor of our culture."

"This is why he's always been a figure of such importance to you. Even though the story itself made no real sense to you, you could identify with Adam as its protagonist. From the beginning, you recognized him as one of your own."

TEN

1

An uncle arrived in town unannounced and expected to be entertained. I thought it would be a day; it turned out to be two and a half. I found myself beaming these thoughts at him: "Isn't it getting to be time for you to move on? Aren't you homesick by now? Wouldn't you rather explore the city on your own? Doesn't it ever occur to you that I might have other things to do?" He was not receptive.

A few minutes before I left to take him to the airport, I

got a call and an ultimatum from a client: No more excuses, not one word—do the work now, or send back the advance. I said I'd do the work now. I took my visiting relative to the airport, came back, and sat down at the word processor. It wasn't that big a chore, I told myself—pointless to make a trip downtown just to tell Ishmael I wasn't going to be there for another day or two.

But in the water of my bones and bowels there was a tremor of apprehension.

I pray about teeth—doesn't everyone? I don't have time to floss. You know. Hang in there, I tell them; I'll get around to you before it's too late. But during the second night a molar that was way, way in the back gave up the ghost. The next morning I found a dentist who agreed to take it out and give it a decent burial. In the chair, while he gave me shot after shot and fiddled with his equipment and checked my blood pressure, I found myself thinking, "Look, I don't have time for this—just yank it out and let me go." But he turned out to be right. Oh my, what roots that tooth had—and it seemed to be a lot closer to my spine than my lips. At one point I asked him if it wouldn't be easier to go in from the back.

When it was over, another side of his personality emerged. He became a Tooth Policeman, and I had been well and truly pulled over to the curb. He scolded me, made me feel small, irresponsible, and immature. I nodded and promised and nodded and promised, thinking, *Please, Officer, give me one more chance, set me loose on my own recognizance.* Eventually he did, but when I got home my hands were shaking and the gauze pads that came out of my jaw weren't pretty. I spent the day gobbling pain-killers and antibiotics and drinking myself silly with bourbon.

In the morning I got back to work, but that tremor of apprehension was still singing in my water.

"One more day," I said to myself. "I'll be able to get this in the mail tonight, and one more day won't matter."

The gambler who puts his last hundred on odd and watches the ball hop decisively into slot 18 will tell you he *knew* it was a losing bet the instant the chip left his hand. He knew it, *felt* it. But of course if it had taken one more hop and landed in 19, he would cheerfully admit that such presentiments often prove to be wrong.

Mine was not.

From the head of the hallway, I saw an industrial-sized floor scrubber parked outside Ishmael's half-open door. Before I could get there, a middle-aged man in a gray uniform backed out and started locking up. I called to him to wait.

"What are you doing?" I asked, somewhat inelegantly, when he was in range of a normal tone of voice.

It didn't really deserve an answer, and he didn't give me one.

"Look," I said, "I know it's none of my business, but would you mind telling me what's going on here?"

He looked at me as if I were a roach he was sure he'd killed a week ago. Nonetheless, he finally worked his mouth a bit and let a few words through: "Getting the place ready for a new tenant."

"Ah," I said. "But, uh, what happened to the old tenant?"

He shrugged indifferently. "Got evicted, I guess. Wasn't paying her rent."

"*Her* rent?" I had momentarily forgotten that Ishmael was not his own caretaker.

He gave me a doubtful look. "Thought you knew the lady."

"No, I knew the uh . . . the uh . . ."

He stood there blinking at me.

"Look," I said again, floundering, "there's probably a note in there for me, or something."

"Ain't nothin' at all in there now, 'cept a bad smell."

"Would you mind if I had a look for myself?"

He turned back to the door and locked it. "You talk to the management about it, okay? I got things to do."

2

"The management," in the person of a receptionist, couldn't think of any reason why I should be given access to that office or anything else, including information of any kind, on any subject, beyond what I already knew: that the tenant had failed to keep up with the rent and had accordingly been evicted. I tried to unnerve her with a piece of truth, but she rejected scornfully my suggestion that a gorilla had once occupied the premises.

"No such animal has ever been kept—or ever will be kept—on any property managed by this firm."

I told her that she could at least tell me if Rachel Sokolow had been the lessor—what harm could that do?

She said, "That's not the point. If your interest was legitimate, you would already know who the lessor was."

This was not your typical receptionist; if I ever need one of my own, I hope I find one like her.

3

There were half a dozen Sokolows in the phone book, but none was named Rachel. There was a Grace, with the right sort of address for the widow of a wealthy Jewish merchant. The next morning, early, I took my car and did a little discreet trespassing to see if the grounds sported a gazebo; they did.

I got the car washed, polished my serious shoes, and dusted off the shoulders of the one suit I maintain in case of weddings and funerals. Then, to be sure of not running into lunch or tea, I waited until two o'clock to make my appearance.

The Beaux-Arts style isn't to everyone's taste, but I happen to like it when it doesn't confuse itself with a wedding cake. The Sokolow mansion looked cool and majestic yet ever-so-slightly whimsical, like royalty on a picnic. After ringing the bell, I had plenty of time to study the front door, a work of art in its own right, a bronze sculpture depicting the Rape of Europa or the Founding of Rome or some damn thing like that. After a while it was opened by a man I would pick for secretary of state just on the basis of his clothes, his looks, and his bearing. He didn't have to say, "Yeah?" or "Well?" He asked my business just by twitching an eyebrow. I told him I wanted to see Mrs. Sokolow. He asked if I had an appointment, knowing full well that I didn't. I knew this was not a guy I could stiff with a statement that it was a personal matter—meaning, none of his business. I decided to open up a little.

"To tell the truth, I'm trying to get in touch with her daughter."

He gave me a leisurely going-over with his eyes. "You're not a friend of hers," he said at last.

"No, frankly, I'm not."

"If you were, you would know that she died almost three months ago."

His words went through me like a dose of ice water.

He twitched another eyebrow, meaning, "Anything else?"

I decided to open up a little more.

"Were you with *Mr.* Sokolow?"

He frowned, letting me know that he doubted the relevance of my inquiry.

"The reason I ask is . . . may I ask your name?"

He doubted the relevance of this inquiry as well, but he decided to humor me. "My name is Partridge."

"Well, Mr. Partridge, the reason I ask is, did you know . . . Ishmael?"

He narrowed his eyes at me.

"To be completely truthful with you, I'm not looking for Rachel, I'm looking for Ishmael. I understand that Rachel more or less took charge of him after her father died."

"How do you come to understand that?" he asked, giving away nothing.

"Mr. Partridge, if you know the answer to that, you'll probably help me," I said, "and if you don't know the answer to it, you probably won't."

It was an elegant point, and he acknowledged it with a nod. Then he asked why I was looking for Ishmael.

"He's missing from his . . . usual place. Evidently he was evicted."

"Someone must have moved him. Helped him."

"Yes," I said. "I don't suppose he walked into Hertz and rented a car."

Partridge ignored my witticism. "I honestly don't know anything, I'm afraid."

"Mrs. Sokolow?"

"If she knew anything, I would know it first."

I believed him but said: "Give me a place to start."

"I don't know of any place to start, now. Now that Miss Sokolow is dead."

I stood there for a while, chewing on it. "What did she die of?"

"You didn't know her at all?"

"Not from Adam."

"Then that's really none of your business," he told me, without rancor, just stating a plain fact.

4

I considered hiring a private investigator. Then I rehearsed in my head the kind of conversation it would take to get started, and decided to skip it. But because I couldn't just up and quit on it, I made a phone call to the local zoo and asked if they happened to have a lowland gorilla in stock. They didn't. I said I happened to have one I needed to get rid of and did they want it, and they said no. I asked if they could suggest someone who *might* want it, and they said no, not really. I asked them what they'd do if they absolutely had to get rid of a gorilla. They said there might be a laboratory or two that would take it as a specimen, but I could tell they weren't really concentrating.

One thing was obvious: Ishmael had some friends I didn't know about—perhaps former pupils. The only way I could think of to reach them was the way *he* had probably reached them—through an ad in the personals:

FRIENDS OF ISHMAEL: Another friend has lost contact. Please call and tell me where he is.

The ad was a mistake, because it gave me an excuse to turn my brain off. I waited for it to appear, then I waited for it to run for a week, then I waited a few more days for a call that didn't come, and in that way two weeks passed during which I didn't lift a finger.

When I finally faced the fact that I wasn't going to get any response to the ad, I had to look for a new heading, and it took me about three minutes to come up with it. I called city hall and was soon talking to the person who would issue a permit to a traveling show if one turned up and wanted to squat on a vacant lot for a week.

Was there one in town at the moment?

No.

Had there been any in the past month?

Yes, the Darryl Hicks Carnival, with nineteen rides, twenty-four games, and a sideshow, had been here and was gone now for a couple weeks or thereabouts.

Anything like a menagerie?

Don't recollect anything like that being listed.

Maybe an animal or two in the sideshow?

Dunno. Possible.

Next stop on its route?

No idea at all.

It didn't matter. A dozen calls tracked it to a town forty miles north, where it had stayed a week and moved on. Assuming it would keep on moving north, I located its next stop and present location with a single call. And yes, it now boasted of having "Gargantua, the world's most famous gorilla"—a critter that I personally knew had been dead for something like forty years.

For you or anyone with reasonably modern equipment, the Darryl Hicks Carnival would have been ninety minutes away, but for me, in a Plymouth that came out the same year as *Dallas,* it was two hours. When I got there, it was a carnival. You know. Carnivals are like bus stations: Some are bigger than others, but they're all alike. The Darryl Hicks was two acres of the usual sleaze masquerading as merriment, full of ugly people, noise, and the stink of beer, cotton candy, and popcorn. I waded through it in search of the sideshow.

I have the impression that sideshows as I remember them from boyhood (or maybe from movies in boyhood) are nearly extinct in the modern carnival world; if so, the Darryl Hicks has elected to ignore the trend. When I arrived, a barker was putting a fire-eater through his paces, but I didn't stay to watch. There was plenty to see inside—the usual collection of monsters, freaks, and geeks, a bottle-biter, a pincushion, a tattooed fat lady, all the rest, which I ignored.

Ishmael was in a dim corner as far from the entrance as it was possible to be, with two ten-year-olds in attendance.

"I'll bet he could tear those bars right out if he wanted to," one observed.

"Yeah," said the other. "But *he* doesn't know that."

I stood there giving him a smoldering look, and he sat there placidly paying no attention to anything until the boys moved off.

As a couple minutes passed, I went on staring and he went on pretending I wasn't there. Then I gave up and said, "Tell me this. Why didn't you ask for help? I know you could have. They don't evict people overnight."

He gave no sign that he'd heard me.

"How the hell do we go about getting you out of here?"

He went on looking through me as if I were just another volume of air.

I said, "Look, Ishmael, are you sore at me or something?"

At last he gave me an eye, but it wasn't a very friendly one. "I didn't invite you to make yourself my patron," he said, "so kindly refrain from patronizing me."

"You want me to mind my own business."

"In a word, yes."

I looked around helplessly. "You mean you actually want to *stay* here?"

Once again Ishmael's eye turned icy.

"All right, all right," I told him. "But what about me?"

"What *about* you?"

"Well, we weren't finished, were we."

"No, we weren't finished."

"So what are you going to do? Do I just become failure number five, or what?"

He sat blinking at me sullenly for a minute or two. Then he said, "There is no need for you to become failure number five. We can go on as before."

At this point a family of five strolled up to have a look at the most famous gorilla in the world: mom, dad, two girls, and a toddler comatose in his mother's arms.

"So we can just go on as before, can we?" I said, and not in a whisper. "That strikes you as feasible, does it?"

The family of visitors suddenly found me much more interesting than "Gargantua," who, after all, was just sitting there looking morose.

I said, "Well, where shall we begin? Do you remember where we left off?"

Intrigued, the visitors turned to see what response this would evoke from Ishmael. When it came, of course, only I could hear it:

"Shut up."

"Shut up? But I thought we were going to go on just as before."

With a grunt, he shuffled to the rear of the cage and gave us all a look at his back. After a minute or so the visitors decided I deserved a dirty look; they gave it to me and ambled off to view the mummified body of a man shot to death in the Mojave around the end of the Civil War.

"Let me take you back," I said.

"No thanks," he replied, turning around but not coming back up to the front of the cage. "Incredible as it may seem to you, I would rather live this way than on anyone's largess, even yours."

"It would only be largess until we worked out something else."

"Something else being what? Doing stunts on the *Tonight* show? A nightclub act?"

"Listen. If I can get in touch with the others, maybe we can work out some kind of joint effort."

"What the devil are you talking about?"

"I'm talking about the people who helped you get this far. You didn't do it by yourself, did you?"

He stared at me balefully from the shadows. "Go away," he snarled. "Just go away and leave me alone."

I went away and left him alone.

5

I hadn't planned for this—or for anything at all, in fact—so I didn't know what to do. I checked into the cheapest motel I could find and went out for a steak and a couple of drinks to think things over. By nine o'clock, I hadn't made any progress, so I went back to the carnival to see what was going on out there. I was in luck, of sorts—a cold front was moving in, and a nasty light rain was sending the merrymakers home with their spirits dampened.

Do you suppose they're still called roustabouts? I didn't ask the one I found closing down the sideshow tent. He looked to be about eighty, and I offered him a ten for the privilege of communing with nature for a while in the person of the gorilla who was no more Gargantua than I was. He didn't appear to consider any of the ethical aspects of the matter but distinctly sneered at the size of the bribe. I added another ten, and he left a light burning by the cage when he hobbled off. There were folding chairs set up on several of the performers' stages, and I dragged one over and sat down.

Ishmael gazed down at me for a few minutes and then asked where we had left off.

"You'd just finished showing me that the story in Genesis that begins with the Fall of Adam and ends with the murder of Abel is not what it's conventionally understood to be by the people of my culture. It's the story of our agricultural revolution as told by some of the earliest victims of that revolution."

"And what remains, do you think?"

"I don't know. Maybe what remains is to bring it all together for me. I don't know what it all adds up to yet."

"Yes, I agree. Let me think for a bit."

6

"What exactly is culture?" Ishmael asked at last. "As the word is commonly used, not in the special sense we've given it for the purposes of these conversations."

It seemed like a hell of a question to ask someone sitting in a carnival sideshow tent, but I did my best to give it some thought. "I'd say it's the sum total of everything that makes a people a people."

He nodded. "And how does that sum total come into existence?"

"I'm not sure what you're getting at. It comes into existence by people living."

"Yes, but sparrows live, and they don't have a culture."

"Okay, I see what you mean. It's an accumulation. The sum total is an accumulation."

"What you're not telling me is how the accumulation comes into being."

"Oh, I see. Okay. The accumulation is the sum total that is passed from one generation to the next. It comes into being when . . . When a species attains a certain order of intelligence, the members of one generation begin to pass along information and techniques to the next. The next generation takes this accumulation, adds its own discoveries and refinements, and passes the total on to the next."

"And this accumulation is what is called culture."

"Yes, I'd say so."

"It's the sum total of what's passed along, of course, not just information and techniques. It's beliefs, assumptions, theories, customs, legends, songs, stories, dances, jokes, superstitions, prejudices, tastes, attitudes. Everything."

"That's right."

"Oddly enough, the order of intelligence needed for the accumulation to begin is not terribly high. Chimpanzees in the wild are already passing along tool-making and tool-using behaviors to their young. I see that this surprises you."

"No. Well . . . I guess I'm surprised that you cite chimpanzees."

"Instead of gorillas?"

"That's right."

Ishmael frowned. "To tell the truth, I have deliberately avoided all field studies of gorilla life. It is a subject I find I do not care to explore."

I nodded, feeling stupid.

"In any case, if chimpanzees have already begun to accumulate knowledge about what works well for chimpanzees, when do you suppose people began to accumulate knowledge about what works well for people?"

"I'd have to assume it began when people began."

"Your paleoanthropologists would agree. Human culture began with human life, which is to say with *Homo habilis*. The people who were *Homo habilis* passed along to their children all they'd learned, and as each generation contributed its mite, there was an accumulation of this knowledge. And who were the heirs to this accumulation?"

"*Homo erectus*?"

"That's right. And the people who were *Homo erectus* passed along this accumulation generation after generation, each adding its mite to the whole. And who were the heirs to this accumulation?"

"*Homo sapiens*."

"Of course. And the heirs of *Homo sapiens* were the people of *Homo sapiens sapiens*, who passed along this accumulation generation after generation, each adding its mite to the whole. And who were the heirs to *this* accumulation?"

"I'd have to say that the various peoples of the Leavers were the heirs."

"Not the Takers? Why is that?"

"Why is that? I don't know. I'd say it's because . . . Obviously there was a total break with the past at the time of the agricultural revolution. There was no break with the past in the various peoples who were migrating to the Americas at this time. There was no break with the past in the various peoples who inhabited New Zealand or Australia or Polynesia."

"What makes you say that?"

"I don't know. It's my impression."

"Yes, but what's the basis for the impression?"

"I think it's this. I don't know what story all these people are enacting, but I can see that they're all enacting the same one. I can't spell the story out as yet, but it's clearly there—in distinction to the story the people of my culture are enacting. Wherever we encounter them, they're always doing much the same sort of thing, always living much the same sort of life—just the way that wherever we encounter *us*, we're always doing much the same sort of thing, always living much the same sort of life."

"But what's the connection between this and the transmittal of that cultural accumulation that mankind made during the first three million years of human life?"

I thought about it for a couple minutes, then said, "This is the connection. The Leavers are still passing that accumulation along in whatever form it came to them. But we're not, because ten thousand years ago the founders of our culture said, 'This is all shit. This is not the way people should live,' and they got rid of it. They obviously *did* get rid of it, because by the time their descendants step into history there's no trace of the attitudes and ideas you encounter among Leaver peoples everywhere. And then too . . ."

"Yes?"

"This is interesting. I've never noticed this before. . . .

Leaver peoples are always conscious of having a tradition that goes back to very ancient times. We have no such consciousness. For the most part, we're a very 'new' people. Every generation is somehow new, more thoroughly cut off from the past than the one that came before."

"What does Mother Culture have to say about this?"

"Ah," I said, and closed my eyes. "Mother Culture says that this is as it should be. There's nothing in the past for us. The past is dreck. The past is something to be put behind us, something to be escaped from."

Ishmael nodded. "So you see: This is how you came to be cultural amnesiacs."

"How do you mean?"

"Until Darwin and the paleontologists came along to tack three million years of human life onto your history, it was assumed in your culture that the birth of man and the birth of your culture were simultaneous events—were in fact the *same* event. What I mean is that the people of your culture thought that man was born *one of you*. It was assumed that farming is as instinctive to man as honey production is to bees."

"Yes, that's the way it seems."

"When the people of your culture encountered the hunter-gatherers of Africa and America, it was thought that these were people who had *degenerated* from the natural, agricultural state, people who had *lost* the arts they'd been born with. The Takers had no idea that they were looking at what they themselves had been before they became agriculturalists. As far as the Takers knew, there *was* no 'before.' Creation had occurred just a few thousand years ago, and Man the Agriculturalist had immediately set about the task of building civilization."

"Yes, that's right."

"Do you see how this came about?"

"How what came about?"

"How it came about that the memory loss of your own

prerevolutionary period was total—so total that you didn't even know it existed."

"No, I don't. I feel like I should, but I don't."

"It was your observation that what Mother Culture teaches is that the past is dreck, is something to be hurried away from."

"Yes."

"And the point I'm making is that apparently this is something she's been teaching you from the very beginning."

"Yes, I see. It's coming together for me now. I was saying that among the Leavers you always have the sense of a people with a past extending back to the dawn of time. Among the Takers you have the sense of a people with a past extending back to 1963."

Ishmael nodded, but then went on: "At the same time, it should be noted that ancientness is a great validator among the people of your culture—so long as it's restricted to that function. For example, the English want all their institutions—and all the pageantry surrounding those institutions—to be as ancient as possible (even if they're not). Nevertheless, they themselves don't live as the ancient Britons lived, and haven't the slightest inclination to do so. Much the same can be said of the Japanese. They esteem the values and traditions of wiser, nobler ancestors and deplore their disappearance, but they have no interest in living the way those wiser, nobler ancestors lived. In short, ancient customs are nice for institutions, ceremonies, and holidays, but Takers don't want to adopt them for everyday living."

"True."

7

"But of course it was not Mother Culture's teaching that *everything* from the past was to be discarded. What was to be saved? What in fact *was* saved?"

"I would say it was information about how to make things, about how to do things."

"Anything related to production was definitely saved. And that's *how things came to be this way*."

"Yes."

"Of course the Leavers save information about production too, though production for its own sake is rarely a feature of their lives. Among the Leavers, people don't have weekly quotas of pots to make or arrowheads to turn out. They're not preoccupied with stepping up their production of hand-axes."

"True."

"So, although they save information about production, most of the information they save is about something else. How would you characterize that information?"

"I'd say you gave away the answer to that question a few minutes ago. I'd say it comes to what works well for them."

"For them? Not for everyone?"

"No. I'm not an anthropology buff, but I've read enough of it to know that the Zuñi don't think their way is the way for everyone, and that the Navajo don't think their way is the way for everyone. Each of them has a way that works well for *them*."

"And that way that works well for them is what they teach their children."

"Yes. And what we teach our children is how to make things. How to make more things and better things."

"Why don't you teach them what works well for people?"

"I'd say it's because we don't *know* what works well for

people. Every generation has to come up with its own version of what works well for people. My parents had their version, which was pretty well useless, and their parents had *their* version, which was pretty well useless, and we're currently working on *our* version, which will probably seem pretty well useless to our own children."

8

"I've let the conversation stray from its course," Ishmael said grumpily and shifted to a new position, rocking the wagon on its springs. "What I wanted you to see is that each Leaver culture is an accumulation of knowledge that reaches back in an unbroken chain to the beginning of human life. This is why it's no great wonder that each of them is a way that works well. Each has been tested and refined over thousands of generations."

"Yes. Something occurs to me."

"Go ahead."

"Give me a minute. This has something to do with . . . the unavailability of knowledge about how people ought to live."

"Take your time."

"Okay," I said a few minutes later. "Back at the beginning, when I said that there was no such thing as certain knowledge about how people ought to live, what I meant was this: *Certain* knowledge is knowledge of the *one right way*. That's what *we* want. That's what Takers want. We don't want to know a way to live that works well. We want to know the *one right way*. And that's what our prophets give us. And that's what our lawgivers give us. Let me think about this. . . . After five or eight thousand years of amnesia, the Takers really didn't know how to live. They really *must* have turned their backs on the past, because all of a sudden, here comes Hammurabi, and everyone says, 'What are these?' and Hammurabi says, 'These, my children, are *laws!*' 'Laws? What are laws?' And Hammurabi says, 'Laws are things that tell you the *one right way* to live.' What am I trying to say?"

"I'm not sure."

"Maybe it's this. When you started talking about our cultural amnesia, I thought you were being metaphorical. Or maybe exaggerating a little to make a point. Because obviously you can't know what those neolithic farmers were thinking. Nevertheless, here's the fact: After a few thousand years, the descendants of these neolithic farmers were scratching their heads and saying, 'Gee, I wonder how people ought to live.' But in that very same time period, the Leavers of the world *hadn't* forgotten how to live. *They* still knew, but the people of my culture had forgotten, had cut themselves off from a tradition that told them how to live. They *needed* a Hammurabi to tell them how to live. They *needed* a Draco and a Solon and a Moses and a Jesus and a Muhammad. And the Leavers didn't, because they had a way—had a whole bunch of ways—that . . . Hold on. I think I've got it."

"Take your time."

"Every one of the Leavers' ways came into being by evolution, by a process of testing that began even before people had a word for it. No one said, 'Okay, let's form a committee to write up a set of laws for us to follow.' None of these cultures were *inventions*. But that's what all *our* lawgivers gave us—inventions. Contrivances. Not things that had proved out over thousands of generations, but rather arbitrary pronouncements about *the one right way* to live. And this is still what's going on. The laws they make in Washington aren't put on the books because they work well—they're put on the books because they represent *the one right way* to live. You may not have an abortion unless the fetus is threatening your life or was put there by a rapist. There are a lot of people who'd like to see the law read that way. Why? Because that's *the one right way* to live. You may drink yourself to death, but if we catch you smoking a marijuana cigarette, it's the slammer for you, baby, because that's *the one right way*. No one gives a damn about whether our laws work well. Working well is beside the point. . . . Again, I'm not sure what I'm getting at."

Ishmael grunted. "You're not necessarily getting at one specific thing. You're exploring a deep complex of ideas, and you can't expect to get to the bottom of it in twenty minutes."

"True."

"However, there is a point I set out to make here before we go on to other things, and I would like to make it."

"Okay."

"You see now that the Takers and the Leavers accumulate two entirely different kinds of knowledge."

"Yes. The Takers accumulate knowledge about what works well for *things*. The Leavers accumulate knowledge about what works well for *people*."

"But not for *all* people. Each Leaver people has a system that works well for them because it *evolved* among them; it was suited to the terrain in which they lived, suited to the climate in which they lived, suited to the biological community in which they lived, suited to their own peculiar tastes, preferences, and vision of the world."

"Yes."

"And this kind of knowledge is called what?"

"I don't know what you mean."

"Someone who knows what works well for people has what?"

"Well . . . wisdom?"

"Of course. Now, you know that the knowledge of what works well for production is what's valued in your culture. In the same way, the knowledge of what works well for people is what's valued in Leaver cultures. And every time the Takers stamp out a Leaver culture, a wisdom ultimately tested since the birth of mankind disappears from the world beyond recall, just as every time they stamp out a species of life, a life form ultimately tested since the birth of life disappears from the world beyond recall."

"Ugly," I said.

"Yes," Ishmael said. "It is ugly."

9

After a few minutes of head-scratching and earlobe-tugging, Ishmael sent me away for the night.

"I'm tired," he explained. "And I'm too cold to think."

ELEVEN

1

The drizzle continued, and when I arrived at noon the next day there wasn't even anyone around to bribe. I had picked up two blankets for Ishmael at an Army-Navy store—and one for myself to keep him in countenance. He accepted them with gruff thanks but seemed glad enough to put them to use. We sat for a while wallowing in our misery, then he reluctantly began.

"Shortly before my departure—I don't remember what

occasioned the question—you asked me when we were going to get to the story enacted by the Leavers."

"Yes, that's right."

"Why are you interested in knowing that story?"

The question nonplussed me. "Why wouldn't I be interested in knowing it?"

"I'm asking what the point is, in your mind. You know that Abel is all but dead."

"Well . . . yes."

"Then why learn the story he was enacting?"

"Again, why *not* learn it?"

Ishmael shook his head. "I don't care to proceed on that basis. The fact that I can't give you reasons for *not* learning something doesn't supply me with a reason for teaching it."

He was clearly in a bad mood. I couldn't blame him, but I couldn't much sympathize either, since it was he who had insisted on having it this way.

He said: "Is it just a matter of curiosity for you?"

"No, I wouldn't say that. You said in the beginning that two stories have been enacted here. I now know one of them. It seems natural that I'd want to know the other one."

"Natural . . ." he said, as if it wasn't a word he much liked. "I wish you could come up with something that has a bit more heft. Something that would give me the feeling I wasn't the only one here who was supposed to be using his brain."

"I'm afraid I don't see what you're getting at."

"I know you don't, and that's what irks me. You've become a passive listener here, turning your brain off when you sit down and turning it on when you get up to leave."

"I don't think that's true."

"Then tell me why it isn't just a waste of time for you to learn a story that is now all but extinguished."

"Well, *I* don't consider it a waste of time."

"That's not good enough. The fact that something is *not a waste of time* does not inspire me to do it."

I shrugged helplessly.

He shook his head, totally disgusted. "You really do think that learning this would be pointless. That's obvious."

"It's not obvious to me."

"Then you think it has a point?"

"Well . . . yes."

"What point?"

"God . . . I *want* to learn it, that's the point."

"No. I won't proceed on that basis. I *want* to proceed, but not if all I'm doing is satisfying your curiosity. Go away and come back when you can give me some authentic reason for going on."

"What would an authentic reason *sound* like? Give me an example."

"All right. Why bother to learn what story is being enacted here by the people of your own culture?"

"Because enacting that story is destroying the world."

"True. But why bother learning it?"

"Because that's obviously something that should be known."

"Known by whom?"

"By everyone."

"Why? That's what I keep coming back to. Why, why, why? Why should your people know what story they're enacting as they destroy the world?"

"So they can *stop* enacting it. So they can see that they're not just blundering as they do what they do. So they can see that they're involved in a megalomaniac fantasy—a fantasy as insane as the Thousand Year Reich."

"That's what makes the story worth knowing?"

"Yes."

"I'm glad to hear it. Now go away and come back when you can explain what makes the other story worth knowing."

"I don't need to go away. I can explain it now."

"Go ahead."

"People can't just *give up* a story. That's what the kids

tried to do in the sixties and seventies. They tried to stop living like Takers, but there was no other way for them to live. They failed because you can't just stop being in a story, you have to have another story to be in."

Ishmael nodded. "And if there is such a story, people should hear about it?"

"Yes, they should."

"Do you think they *want* to hear about it?"

"I don't know. I don't think you can start wanting something till you know it exists."

"Very true."

2

"And what do you suppose this story is about?"

"I have no idea."

"Do you suppose it's about hunting and gathering?"

"I don't know."

"Be honest. Haven't you been expecting some noble paean to the mysteries of the Great Hunt?"

"I'm not aware of expecting anything like that."

"Well, you should at least know that it's about the meaning of the world, about divine intentions in the world, and about the destiny of man."

"Yes."

"As I've said half a dozen times, man *became* man enacting this story. You should remember that."

"Yes, I do."

"How *did* man become man?"

I examined that one for booby traps and gave it back. "I'm not sure what the question means," I said. "Or rather I'm not sure what kind of answer you want. Obviously you don't want me to say that man became man by evolving."

"That would just mean that he became man by becoming man, wouldn't it?"

"Yes."

"So the question is still there waiting to be answered: How did man become man?"

"I suppose it's one of those very obvious things."

"Yes. If I gave you the answer, you'd say, 'Oh. Well of course, but so what?'"

I shrugged, defeated.

"We'll have to approach it obliquely then—but keep it in mind as a question that needs answering."

"Okay."

3

"According to Mother Culture, what kind of event was your agricultural revolution?"

"What *kind* of event . . . I'd say that, according to Mother Culture, it was a technological event."

"No implication of deeper human resonances, cultural or religious?"

"No. The first farmers were just neolithic technocrats. That's the way it's always seemed."

"But after our look at chapters three and four of Genesis, you see there was a great deal more to it than Mother Culture teaches."

"Yes."

"Was and is a great deal more to it, of course, since the revolution is still in progress. Adam is still chewing the fruit of that forbidden tree, and wherever Abel can still be found, Cain is there too, hunting him down, knife in hand."

"That's right."

"There's another indication that the revolution goes deeper than mere technology. Mother Culture teaches that, before the revolution, human life was devoid of meaning, was stupid, empty, and worthless. Prerevolutionary life was ugly. Detestable."

"Yes."

"You believe that yourself, don't you?"

"Yes, I suppose I do."

"Certainly most of you believe it, wouldn't you say?"

"Yes."

"Who would be the exceptions?"

"I don't know. I suppose . . . anthropologists."

"People who actually have some knowledge of that life."

"Yes."

"But Mother Culture teaches that that life was unspeakably miserable."

"That's right."

"Can you imagine any circumstances in which you yourself would trade your life for that sort of life?"

"No. Frankly, I can't imagine why anyone would, given the choice."

"The Leavers would. Throughout history, the only way the Takers have found to tear them away from that life is by brute force, by wholesale slaughter. In most cases, they found it easiest just to exterminate them."

"True. But Mother Culture has something to say about that. What she says is that the Leavers just didn't know what they were missing. They didn't understand the benefits of the agricultural life, and that's why they clung to the hunting-gathering life so tenaciously."

Ishmael smiled his sneakiest smile. "Among the Indians of this country, who would you say were the fiercest and most resolute opponents of the Takers?"

"Well . . . I'd say the Plains Indians."

"I think most of you would agree with that. But before the introduction of horses by the Spanish, the Plains Indians had been agriculturalists for *centuries*. As soon as horses became readily available, they abandoned agriculture and resumed the hunting-gathering life."

"I didn't know that."

"Well, now you do. Did the Plains Indians understand the benefits of the agricultural life?"

"I guess they must have."

"What does Mother Culture say?"

I thought about that for a while, then laughed. "She says they didn't *really* understand. If they had, they would never have gone back to hunting and gathering."

"Because that's a detestable life."

"That's right."

"You can begin to see how thoroughly effective Mother Culture's teachings are on this issue."

"True. But what I don't see is where this gets us."

"We're on our way to discovering what lies at the very root of your fear and loathing of the Leaver life. We're on our way to discovering why you feel you must carry the revolution forward even if it destroys you and the entire world. We're on our way to discovering what your revolution was a revolution *against*."

"Ah," I said.

"And when we've done all that, I'm sure you'll be able to tell me what story was being enacted here by the Leavers during the first three million years of human life and is still being enacted by them wherever they survive today."

4

Having spoken of survival, Ishmael shuddered and sank down into his blankets with a kind of moaning sigh. For a minute he seemed to lose himself in the tireless drumming of rain on the canvas overhead, then he cleared his throat and went on.

"Let's try this," he said. "Why was the revolution *necessary*?"

"It was necessary if man was to get somewhere."

"You mean if man was to have central heating and universities and opera houses and spaceships."

"That's right."

Ishmael nodded. "That sort of answer would have been acceptable when we began our work together, but I want you to go deeper than that now."

"Okay. But I don't know what you mean by deeper."

"You know very well that for hundreds of millions of you, things like central heating, universities, opera houses, and spaceships belong to a remote and unattainable world. Hundreds of millions of you live in conditions that most people in this country can only guess at. Even in this country, millions are homeless or live in squalor and despair in slums, in prisons, in public institutions that are little better than prisons. For these people, your facile justification for the agricultural revolution would be completely meaningless."

"True."

"But though they don't enjoy the fruits of your revolution, would they turn their backs on it? Would they trade their misery and despair for the sort of life that was lived in prerevolutionary times?"

"Again, I'd have to say no."

"This is my impression as well. Takers believe in their revolution, even when they enjoy none of its benefits. There are no grumblers, no dissidents, no counterrevolutionaries. They all believe profoundly that, however bad things are now, they're still infinitely preferable to what came before."

"Yes, I'd say so."

"Today I want you to get to the root of this extraordinary belief. When you've done that, you'll have a completely different understanding of your revolution and of the Leaver life as well."

"Okay. But how do I do that?"

"By listening to Mother Culture. She's been whispering in your ear throughout your life, and what you've heard is no different from what your parents and grandparents heard, from what people all over the world hear daily. In other words, what I'm looking for is buried in your mind just as it's buried in all your minds. Today I want you to unearth it. Mother Culture has taught you to have a horror of the life you put behind you with your revolution, and I want you to trace this horror to its roots."

"Okay," I said. "It's true that we have something amounting to a horror of that life, but the trouble is, this just doesn't seem particularly mysterious to me."

"It doesn't? Why?"

"I don't know. It's a life that leads nowhere."

"No more of these superficial answers. Dig."

With a sigh, I scrunched down inside my blanket and proceeded to dig. "This is interesting," I said a few minutes later. "I was sitting here thinking about the way our ancestors lived, and a very specific image popped into my head fully formed."

Ishmael waited for me to go on.

"It has a sort of dreamlike quality to it. Or nightmarish. A man is scrabbling along a ridge at twilight. In this world it's always twilight. The man is short, thin, dark, and naked. He's running in a half crouch, looking for tracks. He's hunting, and he's desperate. Night is falling and he's got nothing to eat.

"He's running and running and running, as if he were on a treadmill. It *is* a treadmill, because tomorrow at twilight he'll be there running still—or running again. But there's more than hunger and desperation driving him. He's terrified as well. Behind him on the ridge, just out of sight, his enemies are in pursuit to tear him to pieces—the lions, the wolves, the tigers. And so he has to stay on that treadmill forever, forever one step behind his prey and one step ahead of his enemies.

"The ridge, of course, represents the knife-edge of survival. The man lives on the knife-edge of survival and has to struggle perpetually to keep from falling off. Actually it's as though the ridge and the sky are in motion instead of him. He's running in place, trapped, going nowhere."

"In other words, hunter-gatherers lead a very grim life."

"Yes."

"And why is it grim?"

"Because it's a struggle just to stay alive."

"But in fact it isn't anything of the kind. I'm sure you know that, in another compartment of your mind. Hunter-gatherers no more live on the knife-edge of survival than wolves or lions or sparrows or rabbits. Man was as well adapted to life on this planet as any other species, and the idea that he lived on the knife-edge of survival is simply biological nonsense. As an omnivore, his dietary range is immense. Thousands of species will go hungry before he does. His intelligence and dexterity enable him to live comfortably in conditions that would utterly defeat any other primate.

"Far from scrabbling endlessly and desperately for food, hunter-gatherers are among the best-fed people on earth, and they manage this with only two or three hours a day of what you would call work—which makes them among the most leisured people on earth as well. In his book on stone age economics, Marshall Sahlins described them as 'the original affluent society.' And incidentally, predation of man is practically nonexistent. He's simply not the first choice on any predator's menu. So you see that your wonderfully horrific vision of your ancestors' life is just another bit of Mother Culture's nonsense. If you like, you can confirm all this for yourself in an afternoon at the library."

"Okay," I said. "So?"

"So now that you know that it's nonsense, do you feel differently about that life? Does it seem less repulsive to you?"

"Less repulsive maybe. But still repulsive."

"Consider this. Let's suppose you're one of this nation's

homeless. Out of work, no skills, a wife the same, two kids. Nowhere to turn, no hope, no future. But I can give you a box with a button on it. Press the button and you'll all be whisked instantly back to prerevolutionary times. You'll all be able to speak the language, you'll all have the skills everyone had then. You'll never again have to worry about taking care of yourself and your family. You'll have it made, you'll be a part of that original affluent society."

"Okay."

"So, do you press the button?"

"I don't know. I have to doubt it."

"Why? It isn't that you'd be giving up a wonderful life here. According to this hypothesis, the life you've got here is wretched, and it's not likely to improve. So it has to be that the other life seems even worse. It isn't that you couldn't bear giving up the life you've got—it's that you couldn't bear embracing that other life."

"Yes, that's right."

"What is it that makes that life so horrifying to you?"

"I don't know."

"It seems that Mother Culture has done a good job on you."

"Yes."

"All right. Let's try this. Wherever the Takers have come up against some hunter-gatherers taking up space they wanted for themselves, they've tried to explain to them why they should abandon their life-style and become Takers. They've said, 'This life of yours is not only wretched, it's wrong. Man was not meant to live this way. So don't fight us. Join our revolution and help us turn the world into a paradise for man.'"

"Right."

"You take that part—the part of the cultural missionary—and I'll take the part of a hunter-gatherer. Explain to me why the life that I and my people have found satisfying for thousands of years is grim and revolting and repulsive."

"Good lord."

"Look, I'll get you started. . . . Bwana, you tell us that the way we live is wretched and wrong and shameful. You tell us that it's not the way people are meant to live. This puzzles us, Bwana, because for thousands of years it has seemed to us a good way to live. But if you, who ride to the stars and send your words around the world at the speed of thought, tell us that it isn't, then we must in all prudence listen to what you have to say."

"Well . . . I realize it seems good to you. This is because you're ignorant and uneducated and stupid."

"Exactly so, Bwana. We await your enlightenment. Tell us why our life is wretched and squalid and shameful."

"Your life is wretched and squalid and shameful because you live like animals."

Ishmael frowned, puzzled. "I don't understand, Bwana. We live as all others live. We take what we need from the world and leave the rest alone, just as the lion and the deer do. Do the lion and the deer lead shameful lives?"

"No, but that's because they're just animals. It's not right for humans to live that way."

"Ah," Ishmael said, "this we did not know. And why is it not right to live that way?"

"It's because, living that way . . . you have no control over your lives."

Ishmael cocked his head at me. "In what sense do we have no control over our lives, Bwana?"

"You have no control over the most basic necessity of all, your food supply."

"You puzzle me greatly, Bwana. When we're hungry, we go off and find something to eat. What more control is needed?"

"You'd have more control if you planted it yourself."

"How so, Bwana? What does it matter who plants the food?"

"If you plant it yourself, then you know positively that it's going to be there."

Ishmael cackled delightedly. "Truly you astonish me, Bwana! We *already* know positively that it's going to be there. The whole world of life is food. Do you think it's going to sneak away during the night? Where would it go? It's always there, day after day, season after season, year after year. If it weren't, we wouldn't be here to talk to you about it."

"Yes, but if you planted it yourself, you could control *how much* food there was. You'd be able to say, 'Well, this year we'll have more yams, this year we'll have more beans, this year we'll have more strawberries.'"

"Bwana, these things grow in abundance without the slightest effort on our part. Why should we trouble ourselves to plant what is already growing?"

"Yes, but . . . don't you ever run out? Don't you ever wish you had a yam but find there are no more growing wild?"

"Yes, I suppose so. But isn't it the same for you? Don't you ever wish you had a yam but find there are no more growing in your fields?"

"No, because if we wish we had a yam, we can go to the store and buy a can of them."

"Yes, I have heard something of this system. Tell me this, Bwana. The can of yams that you buy in the store—how many of you labored to put that can there for you?"

"Oh, hundreds, I suppose. Growers, harvesters, truckers, cleaners at the canning plant, people to run the equipment, people to pack the cans in cases, truckers to distribute the cases, people at the store to unpack them, and so on."

"Forgive me, but you sound like lunatics, Bwana, to do all this work just to ensure that you can never be disappointed over the matter of a yam. Among my people, when we want a yam, we simply go and dig one up—and if there are none to be found, we find something else just as good, and hundreds of people don't need to labor to put it into our hands."

"You're missing the point."

"I certainly am, Bwana."

I stifled a sigh. "Look, here's the point. Unless you control your own food supply, you live at the mercy of the world. It doesn't matter that there's always been enough. That's not the point. You can't live at the whim of the gods. That's just not a human way to live."

"Why is that, Bwana?"

"Well . . . look. One day you go out hunting, and you catch a deer. Okay, that's fine. That's terrific. But you didn't have any control over the deer's being there, did you?"

"No, Bwana."

"Okay. The next day you go out hunting and there's no deer to be caught. Hasn't that ever happened?"

"Assuredly, Bwana."

"Well, there you are. Because you have no control over the deer, you have no deer. So what do you do?"

Ishmael shrugged. "We snare a couple of rabbits."

"Exactly. You shouldn't have to settle for rabbits if what you want is deer."

"And this is why we lead shameful lives, Bwana? This is why we should set aside a life we love and go to work in one of your factories? Because we eat rabbits when it happens that no deer presents itself to us?"

"No. Let me finish. You have no control over the deer— and no control over the rabbits either. Suppose you go out hunting one day, and there are no deer *and* no rabbits? What do you do then?"

"Then we eat something else, Bwana. The world is full of food."

"Yes, but look. If you have no control over *any* of it . . ." I bared my teeth at him. "Look, there's no guarantee that the world is *always* going to be full of food, is there? Haven't you ever had a drought?"

"Certainly, Bwana."

"Well, what happens then?"

"The grasses wither, all the plants wither. The trees bear no fruit. The game disappears. The predators dwindle."

"And what happens to you?"

"If the drought is very bad, then we too dwindle."

"You mean you *die*, don't you?"

"Yes, Bwana."

"Ha! *That's* the point!"

"It's shameful to *die*, Bwana?"

"No. . . . I've got it. Look, this is the point. You die because you live at the mercy of the gods. You die because you think the gods are going to look after you. That's okay for animals, but you should know better."

"We should not trust the gods with our lives?"

"Definitely not. You should trust *yourselves* with your lives. That's the human way to live."

Ishmael shook his head ponderously. "This is sorry news indeed, Bwana. From time out of mind we've lived in the hands of the gods, and it seemed to us we lived well. We left to the gods all the labor of sowing and growing and lived a carefree life, and it seemed there was always enough in the world for us, because—behold!—*we are here*!"

"Yes," I told him sternly. "You are here, and look at you. You have nothing. You're naked and homeless. You live without security, without comfort, without opportunity."

"And this is because we live in the hands of the gods?"

"Absolutely. In the hands of the gods you're no more important than lions or lizards or fleas. In the hands of *these* gods—these gods who look after lions and lizards and fleas—you're nothing special. You're just another animal to be fed. Wait a second," I said, and closed my eyes for a couple minutes. "Okay, this is important. The gods make no distinction between you and any other creature. No, that's not quite it. Hold on." I went back to work, then tried again. "Here it is: What the gods provide is enough for your life as *animals*—I grant you that. But for your life as humans, *you* must provide. The gods are not going to do that."

Ishmael gave me a stunned look. "You mean there is something we need that the gods are not willing to give us, Bwana?"

"That's the way it seems, yes. They give you what you need to live as animals but not what you need *beyond that* to live as humans."

"But how can that be, Bwana? How can it be that the gods are wise enough to shape the universe and the world and the life of the world but lack the wisdom to give humans what they need to be human?"

"I don't know how it can be, but it is. That's the fact. Man lived in the hands of the gods for three million years and at the end of those three million years was no better off and no farther ahead than when he started."

"Truly, Bwana, this is strange news. What kind of gods *are* these?"

I snorted a laugh. "These, my friend, are *incompetent* gods. This is why you've got to take your lives out of their hands entirely. You've got to take your lives into your *own* hands."

"And how do we do that, Bwana?"

"As I say, you've got to begin planting your own food."

"But how will that change anything, Bwana? Food is food, whether we plant it or the gods plant it."

"That's exactly the point. The gods plant only what you *need*. You will plant *more* than you need."

"To what end, Bwana? What's the good of having more food than we need?"

"*Damn!*" I shouted. "I get it!"

Ishmael smiled and said, "So what's the good of having more food than we need?"

"That is the whole goddamned point! When you have

more food than you need, then *the gods have no power over you!*"

"We can thumb our noses at them."

"Exactly."

"All the same, Bwana, what are we to *do* with this food if we don't need it?"

"You *save* it! You save it to thwart the gods when they decide it's your turn to go hungry. You save it so that when they send a drought, you can say, 'Not *me,* goddamn it! *I'm* not going hungry, and there's nothing you can do about it, because my life is in my own hands now!'"

5

Ishmael nodded, abandoning his hunter-gatherer role. "So your lives are now in your own hands."

"That's right."

"Then what are you all so worried about?"

"What do you mean?"

"If your lives are in your own hands, then it's entirely up to you whether you go on living or become extinct. That's what this expression means, isn't it?"

"Yes. But obviously there are still some things that *aren't* in our hands. We wouldn't be able to control or survive a total ecological collapse."

"So you're not safe yet. When will you finally be safe?"

"When we've taken the *whole world* out of the hands of the gods."

"When the whole world is in your own, more competent, hands."

"That's right. Then the gods will finally have no more power over us. Then the gods will have no more power over *anything.* All the power will be in our hands and we'll be free at last."

6

"Well," Ishmael said, "are we making progress?"

"I think so."

"Do you think we've found the root of your revulsion toward the sort of life that was lived in prerevolutionary times?"

"Yes. Far and away the most futile admonition Christ ever offered was when he said, 'Have no care for tomorrow. Don't worry about whether you're going to have something to eat. Look at the birds of the air. They neither sow nor reap nor gather into barns, but God takes perfect care of them. Don't you think he'll do the same for you?' In our culture the overwhelming answer to that question is, 'Hell no!' Even the most dedicated monastics saw to their sowing and reaping and gathering into barns."

"What about Saint Francis?"

"Saint Francis relied on the bounty of farmers, not the bounty of God. Even the most fundamental of the fundamentalists plug their ears when Jesus starts talking about birds of the air and lilies of the field. They know damn well he's just yarning, just making pretty speeches."

"So you think this is what's at the root of your revolution. You wanted and still want to have your lives in your own hands."

"Yes. Absolutely. To me, living any other way is almost inconceivable. I can only think that hunter-gatherers live in a state of utter and unending anxiety over what tomorrow's going to bring."

"Yet they don't. Any anthropologist will tell you that. They are far less anxiety-ridden than you are. They have no jobs to lose. No one can say to them, 'Show me your money or you don't get fed, don't get clothed, don't get sheltered.'"

"I believe you. Rationally speaking, I believe you. But I'm talking about my feelings, about my conditioning. My conditioning tells me—Mother Culture tells me—that living in the hands of the gods has got to be a never-ending nightmare of terror and anxiety."

"And this is what your revolution does for you: It puts you beyond the reach of that appalling nightmare. It puts you beyond the reach of the gods."

"Yes, that's it."

"So. We have a new pair of names for you. The Takers are those who know good and evil, and the Leavers are . . . ?"

"The Leavers are those who live in the hands of the gods."

TWELVE

1

Along about three o'clock, the rain stopped and the carnival yawned, stretched, and went back to work separating the rubes from their money. At loose ends once again, I hung around for a while, let myself be separated from a few bucks, and finally had the idea of tracking down Ishmael's owner. This turned out to be a hard-eyed black man named Art Owens, who was five and a half feet tall and spent more time lifting weights than I do at the typewriter. I told him I was interested in buying his gorilla.

"Is that a fact," he said, not scornful, not impressed, not interested, not anything.

I told him it was and asked how much it would take.

"Would take about three thousand."

"I'm not that interested."

"How interested are you?" Just curious, not seriously interested himself.

"Well, more like a thousand."

He sneered—just a little, almost politely. For some reason, I liked this guy. He was the type who has a law degree from Harvard stuck away in a drawer somewhere because he never found anything to do with it that appealed to him.

I told him: "This is a very, very old animal, you know. The Johnsons brought him over in the thirties."

This got his attention. He asked how I happened to come by that piece of information.

"I know the animal," I replied briefly, as if I might know thousands more like him.

"Might go twenty-five hundred," he said.

"Trouble is, I don't *have* twenty-five hundred."

"See, I already got a painter in New Mexico workin' on a sign for me," he said. "Paid him two hundred in advance."

"Uh huh. I could probably raise fifteen hundred."

"Don't see how I could go below twenty-two, that's a fact."

The fact was, if it was right there in my hand, he'd be delighted to take two thousand. Maybe even eighteen hundred. I said I'd think about it.

2

It was a Friday night, so the suckers didn't start going home till after eleven and my senectuous bribee didn't come round to collect his twenty dollars till midnight. Ishmael was asleep sitting up, still bundled up in his blankets, and I didn't feel any qualms about waking him; I wanted him to reassess the charms of the independent life.

He yawned, sneezed twice, cleared his throat of a mass of phlegm, and fixed me in a bleary, malevolent glare.

"Come back tomorrow," he said in the equivalent of a mental croak.

"Tomorrow's Saturday—hopeless."

He wasn't happy about it, but he knew I was right. He managed to put off the inevitable by laboriously rearranging himself, his cage, and his blankets. Then he settled down and gave me a look of loathing.

"Where did we leave off?"

"We left off with a new pair of names for the Takers and the Leavers: Those who know good and evil and those who live in the hands of the gods."

He grunted.

3

"What *happens* to people who live in the hands of the gods?"

"What do you mean?"

"I mean, what happens to people who live in the hands of the gods that does *not* happen to people who build their lives on the knowledge of good and evil?"

"Well, let's see," I said. "I don't suppose this is what you're getting at, but this is what comes to mind. People who live in the hands of the gods don't make themselves rulers of the world and force everyone to live the way they live, and people who know good and evil do."

"You've turned the question round back to front," said Ishmael. "I asked what happens to people who live in the hands of the gods that *doesn't* happen to those who know good and evil, and you told me just the opposite: what *doesn't* happen to people who live in the hands of the gods that *does* happen to those who know good and evil."

"You mean you're looking for something *positive* that happens to people who live in the hands of the gods."

"That's right."

"Well, they do tend to let the people around them live the way they want to live."

"You're telling me something they *do*, not something that *happens* to them. I'm trying to focus your attention on the effects of this life-style."

"I'm sorry. I'm afraid I just don't know what you're getting at."

"You do, but you're not used to thinking about it in these terms."

"Okay."

"You remember the question we started out to answer when you arrived this afternoon: How did man become man? We're still after the answer to that question."

I groaned, fully and frankly.

"Why do you groan?" Ishmael asked.

"Because questions of that generality intimidate me. How did man become man? I don't know. He just did it. He did it the way birds became birds and the way that horses became horses."

"Exactly so."

"Don't do that to me," I told him.

"Evidently you don't understand what you just said."

"Probably not."

"I'll try to clarify it for you. Before you were *Homo*, you were what?"

"*Australopithecus.*"

"Good. And how did *Australopithecus* become *Homo*?"

"By waiting."

"Please. You're here to think."

"Sorry."

"Did *Australopithecus* become *Homo* by saying, 'We know good and evil as well as the gods, so there's no need for us to live in their hands the way rabbits and lizards do.

From now on *we* will decide who lives and who dies on this planet, not the gods.'"

"No."

"*Could* they have become man by saying that?"

"No."

"Why not?"

"Because they would have ceased to be subject to the conditions under which evolution takes place."

"Exactly. Now you can answer the question: What happens to people—to creatures in general—who live in the hands of the gods?"

"Ah. Yes, I see. They evolve."

"And now you can answer the question I posed this morning: How did man become man?"

"Man became man by living in the hands of the gods."

"By living the way the Bushmen of Africa live."

"That's right."

"By living the way the Kreen-Akrore of Brazil live."

"Right again."

"Not the way Chicagoans live?"

"No."

"Or Londoners?"

"No."

"So now you know what happens to people who live in the hands of the gods."

"Yes. They evolve."

"Why do they evolve?"

"Because they're in a *position* to evolve. Because that's where evolution takes place. Pre-man evolved into early man because he was out there competing with all the rest. Pre-man evolved into early man because he didn't take himself out of the competition, because he was still in the place where natural selection is going on."

"You mean he was still a part of the general community of life."

"That's right."

"And that's why it all happened—why *Australopithecus* became *Homo habilis* and why *Homo habilis* became *Homo erectus* and why *Homo erectus* became *Homo sapiens* and why *Homo sapiens* became *Homo sapiens sapiens*."

"Yes."

"And then what happened?"

"And then the Takers said, 'We've had enough of living in the hands of the gods. No more natural selection for us, thanks very much.'"

"And that was that."

"And that was that."

"You remember I said that to enact a story is to live so as to make it come true."

"Yes."

"According to the Taker story, creation came to an end with man."

"Yes. So?"

"How would you live so as to make *that* come true? How would you live so as to make creation come to an end with man?"

"Oof. I see what you mean. You would live the way the Takers live. We're definitely living in a way that's going to put an end to creation. If we go on, there will be no successor to man, no successor to chimpanzees, no successor to orangutans, no successor to gorillas—no successor to anything alive now. The whole thing is going to come to an end with us. In order to make their story come true, the Takers have to put an end to creation itself—and they're doing a damned good job of it."

4

"When we began and I was trying to help you find the premise of the Taker story, I told you that the Leaver story has an entirely different premise."

"Yes."

"Perhaps you're ready to articulate that premise now."

"I don't know. At the moment I can't even think of the Taker premise."

"It'll come back to you. Every story is a working out of a premise."

"Yes, okay. The premise of the Taker story is *the world belongs to man*." I thought for a couple of minutes, then I laughed. "It's almost too neat. The premise of the Leaver story is *man belongs to the world*."

"Meaning what?"

"Meaning—" I barked a laugh. "It's really too much."

"Go on."

"It means that, right from the beginning, everything that ever lived belonged to the world—and that's *how things came to be this way*. Those single-celled creatures that swam in the ancient oceans belonged to the world, and because they did, everything that followed came into being. Those club-finned fish offshore of the continents belonged to world, and because they did, the amphibians eventually came into being. And because the amphibians belonged to the world, the reptiles eventually came into being. And because the reptiles belonged to the world, the mammals eventually came into being. And because the mammals belonged to the world, the primates eventually came into being. And because the primates belonged to the world, *Australopithecus* eventually came into being. And because *Australopithecus* belonged to the world, man eventually came into being. And for three million years man belonged to the world—and *because* he belonged to the world, he grew and developed and became brighter and more dexterous until one day he was so bright and dexterous that we had to call him *Homo sapiens sapiens,* which means that he was *us.*"

"And that's the way the Leavers lived for three million years—as if they belonged to the world."

"That's right. And that's how *we* came into being."

5

Ishmael said, "We know what happens if you take the Taker premise, that the world belongs to man."

"Yes, that's a disaster."

"And what happens if you take the Leaver premise, that man belongs to the world?"

"Then creation goes on forever."

"How does that sound?"

"It has my vote."

6

"Something occurs to me," I said.

"Yes?"

"It occurs to me that the story I just told is in fact the story the Leavers have been enacting here for three million years. The Takers' story is, 'The gods made the world for man, but they botched the job, so we had to take matters into our own, more competent hands.' The Leavers' story is, 'The gods made man for the world, the same way they made salmon and sparrows and rabbits for the world; this seems to have worked pretty well so far, so we can take it easy and leave the running of the world to the gods.'"

"That's right. There are other ways to tell it, just as there are other ways to tell the story of the Takers, but this way of telling it is as good as any."

I sat there for a while. "I'm thinking about . . . the meaning of the world, divine intentions in the world, and the destiny of man. According to this story."

"Go ahead."

"The meaning of the world . . . I think the third chapter of Genesis had it right. It's a garden—the gods' garden. I say this even though I myself very much doubt that gods have anything to do with it. I just find this a wholesome and encouraging way to think of it."

"I understand."

"And there are two trees in the garden, one for the gods and one for us. The one for them is the Tree of the Knowledge of Good and Evil, and the one for us is the Tree of Life. But we can only find the Tree of Life if we stay in the garden—and we can only stay in the garden if we keep our hands off the gods' tree."

Ishmael gave me a nod of encouragement.

"Divine intentions . . . It would seem . . . There is a sort of tendency in evolution, wouldn't you say? If you start with those ultrasimple critters in the ancient seas and move up step by step to everything we see here now—and beyond—then you have to observe a tendency toward . . . complexity. And toward self-awareness and intelligence. Wouldn't you agree?"

"Yes."

"That is, all sorts of creatures on this planet appear to be on the verge of attaining that self-awareness and intelligence. So it's definitely not just humans that the gods are after. We were never meant to be the only players on this stage. Apparently the gods intend this planet to be a garden *filled* with creatures that are self-aware and intelligent."

"So it would appear. And if this is so, then man's destiny would seem to be plain."

"Yes. Amazingly enough, it *is* plain—because man is the

first of all these. He's the trailblazer, the pathfinder. His destiny is to be the first to learn that creatures like man have a choice: They can try to thwart the gods and perish in the attempt—or they can stand aside and make some room for all the rest. But it's more than that. His destiny is to be the father of them all—I don't mean by direct descent. By giving all the rest their chance—the whales and the dolphins and the chimps and the raccoons—he becomes in some sense their progenitor. . . . Oddly enough, it's even grander than the destiny the Takers dreamed up for us."

"How so?"

"Just think. In a billion years, whatever is around then, *whoever* is around then, says, 'Man? Oh yes, *man*! What a wonderful creature he was! It was within his grasp to destroy the entire world and to trample all our futures into the dust—but he saw the light before it was too late and pulled back. He pulled back and gave the rest of us our chance. He showed us all how it *had to be done* if the world was to go on being a garden forever. Man was the role model for us all!'"

"Not a shabby destiny."

"Not a shabby destiny by any means. And it occurs to me that this . . ."

"Yes?"

"This gives a little shape to the story. The world is a very, very fine place. It wasn't a mess. It didn't need to be conquered and ruled by man. In other words, the world doesn't need to belong to man—but it *does* need man to belong to *it*. *Some* creature had to be the first to go through this, had to see that there were two trees in the garden, one that was good for gods and one that was good for creatures. *Some* creature had to find the way, and if that happened, then . . . there was just no limit to what could happen here. In other words, man does have a place in the world, but it's not his place to *rule*. The gods have that in hand. Man's place is to be the first. Man's place is to be the first *without being the last*. Man's place is to figure out how it's *possible* to do that—and then to make some room for all the rest who are capable of becoming what he's become. And maybe, when the time comes, it's man's place to be the teacher of all the rest who are capable of becoming what he's become. Not the only teacher, not the ultimate teacher. Maybe only the first teacher, the kindergarten teacher—but even that wouldn't be too shabby. And do you know what?"

"What?"

"All along, I've been saying to myself, 'Yes, this is all very interesting, but what good is it? This isn't going to change anything!'"

"And now?"

"*This* is what we need. Not just *stopping* things. Not just *less* of things. People need something positive to work for. They need a vision of something that . . . I don't know. Something that . . ."

"I think what you're groping for is that people need more than to be scolded, more than to be made to feel stupid and guilty. They need more than a vision of doom. They need a vision of the world and of themselves that inspires them."

"Yes. Definitely. Stopping pollution is not inspiring. Sorting your trash is not inspiring. Cutting down on fluorocarbons is not inspiring. But this . . . thinking of ourselves in a new way, thinking of the world in a new way . . . This . . ."

I let it go. What the hell, he knew what I was trying to say.

7

"I trust you now see a point I made when we first began. The story being enacted here by the Takers is not in any sense chapter two of the story that was being enacted here during the first three million years of human life. The Leaver story has its own chapter two."

"What *is* its chapter two?"

"You've just outlined it, haven't you?"

"I'm not sure."

Ishmael spent a moment in thought. "We'll never know what the Leavers of Europe and Asia were up to when the people of your culture came along to plow them under forever. But we do know what they were up to here in North America. They were looking for ways to achieve settlement that were in accord with the way they'd always lived, ways that left room for the rest of life to go on around them. I don't mean that they did this out of any sense of high-mindedness. I simply mean that it didn't occur to them to take the life of the world into their own hands and to declare war on the rest of the community of life. Proceeding in this way for another five thousand years or ten thousand years, a dozen civilizations might have appeared on this continent as sophisticated as yours is now, each with its own values and objectives. It's not unthinkable."

"No, it's not. Or rather, yes it is. According to Taker mythology, every civilization anywhere in the universe must be a *Taker* civilization, a civilization in which people have taken the life of the world into their own hands. That's so obvious it doesn't need to be pointed out. Hell, every alien civilization in the history of science fiction has been a Taker civilization. Every civilization ever encountered by the U.S.S. *Enterprise* has been a Taker civilization. This is because it goes without saying that any intelligent creature anywhere will insist on taking his life out of the hands of the gods, will know that the world belongs to him and not the other way around."

"True."

"Which raises an important question in my mind. What exactly would it *mean* to belong to the world at this point? Obviously you're not saying that only hunter-gatherers truly belong to the world."

"I'm glad you see that. Though if the Bushmen of Africa

or the Kalapalo of Brazil (if there are any left by now) want to go on living that way for the next ten million years, I can't see how this can be anything less than beneficial for them and for the world."

"True. But that doesn't answer my question. How can civilized people belong to the world?"

Ishmael shook his head in what looked like a mixture of impatience and exasperation. "Civilized has nothing to do with it. How can tarantulas belong to the world? How can sharks belong to the world?"

"I don't understand."

"Look around you and you'll see some creatures who act as though the world belongs to them and some creatures who act as though they belong to the world. Can you tell them apart?"

"Yes."

"The creatures who act as though they belong to the world follow the peace-keeping law, and because they follow that law, they give the creatures around them a chance to grow toward whatever it's possible for them to become. That's how man came into being. The creatures around *Australopithecus* didn't imagine that the world belonged to them, so they let him live and grow. How does being civilized come into it? Does being civilized mean that you *have* to destroy the world?"

"No."

"Does being civilized make you *incapable* of giving the creatures around you a little space in which to live?"

"No."

"Does it make you incapable of living as harmlessly as sharks and tarantulas and rattlesnakes?"

"No."

"Does it make you incapable of following a law that even snails and earthworms manage to follow without any difficulty?"

"No."

"As I pointed out some time ago, human settlement isn't *against* the law, it's *subject* to the law—and the same is true of civilization. So what exactly is your question?"

"I don't know, now. Obviously belonging to the world means . . . belonging to the same club as everyone else. The club being the community of life. It means belonging to the club and following the same rules as everyone else."

"And if being civilized means anything at all, it should mean that you're leaders of the club, not its only criminals and destroyers."

"True," I said, and then sat there blinking for a few moments. "Something you said a moment ago. We'll never know what the Leavers of Europe or Asia were up to when the people of my culture arrived to plow them under."

"Yes?"

"I think some information about that *has* been dug up in recent years."

Ishmael nodded. "If it's recent, then I might well not have heard of it."

"An archeologist named Riane Eisler wrote about a wide-spread Leaver agricultural society that existed in Europe until it was overrun by the Takers five or six thousand years ago. Except she didn't call them Leavers and Takers, of course. I don't know a lot about it, but evidently the culture the Takers plowed under was based on goddess worship."

Ishmael nodded. "One of my students was aware of the book you're talking about but was unable to explain its significance as you've done. It's called, I believe, *The Chalice and the Blade*."

8

"Returning to the subject of inspiration, it seems to me that these days you have another promising source of it," Ishmael said.

"What's that?"

"All my other pupils, when they reached this point, said, 'Yes, yes, this is wonderful—but people are not going to relinquish their hold on the world. It just can't happen. Never. Not in a thousand years.' And I had nothing I could point to as a hopeful example to the contrary. Now I do."

It took me about ninety seconds to see it. "I assume you mean what's been happening in the Soviet Union and eastern Europe in the past few years."

"That's right. Ten years ago, twenty years ago, anyone predicting that Marxism would soon be dismantled *from the top* would have been labeled a hopeless visionary, an utter fool."

"Yes, that's true."

"But once the people of these countries were inspired by the possibility of a new way of life, the dismantling took place almost overnight."

"Yes, I see what you mean. Five years ago I would have said that no amount of inspiration could accomplish that—or this."

"And now?"

"And now it's just barely thinkable. Improbable as hell but not unimaginable."

9

"But I do have another question," I added.

"Proceed."

"Your ad said, 'Must earnestly desire to save the world.'"

"Yes?"

"What do I do if I earnestly desire to save the world?"

Ishmael frowned at me through the bars for a long moment. "You want a program?"

"Of course I want a program."

"Then here is a program: The story of Genesis must be reversed. First, Cain must stop murdering Abel. This is essential if you're to survive. The Leavers are the endangered species most critical to the world—not because they're humans but because they alone can show the destroyers of the world that there is no *one right way* to live. And then, of course, you must spit out the fruit of that forbidden tree. You must absolutely and forever relinquish the idea that you know who should live and who should die on this planet."

"Yes, I see all that, but that's a program for *mankind*, that's not a program for *me*. What do *I* do?"

"What you do is to teach a hundred what I've taught you, and inspire each of them to teach a hundred. That's how it's always done."

"Yes, but . . . is it *enough*?"

Ishmael frowned. "Of course it's not enough. But if you begin anywhere else, there's no hope at all. You can't say, 'We're going to change the way people behave toward the world, but we're not going to change the way they think about the world or the way they think about divine intentions in the world or the way they think about the destiny of man.' As long as the people of your culture are convinced that the world belongs to them and that their divinely-appointed destiny is to conquer and rule it, then they are of course going to go on acting the way they've been acting for the past ten thousand years. They're going to go on treating the world as if it were a piece of human property and they're going to go on conquering it as if it were an adversary. You can't change these things with *laws*. You must change people's *minds*. And you can't just root out a harmful complex of ideas and leave a void behind; you have to give people something that is as meaningful as what they've lost—something that makes better sense than the old horror of Man Supreme, wiping out everything on this planet that doesn't serve his needs directly or indirectly."

I shook my head. "What you're saying is that someone has to stand up and become to the world of today what Saint Paul was to the Roman Empire."

"Yes, basically. Is that so daunting?"

I laughed. "Daunting isn't nearly strong enough. To call it daunting is like calling the Atlantic damp."

"Is it really so impossible in an age when a stand-up comic on television reaches more people in ten minutes than Paul did in his entire lifetime?"

"I'm not a stand-up comic."

"But you're a writer, aren't you?"

"Not that kind of writer."

Ishmael shrugged. "Lucky you. You are absolved of any obligation. Self-absolved."

"I didn't say that."

"What were you expecting to learn from me? An incantation? A magic word that would sweep all the nastiness away?"

"No."

"Ultimately, it would seem you're no different from those you profess to despise: You just wanted something for yourself. Something to make you feel better as you watch the end approach."

"No, it isn't that. You just don't know me very well. It's always this way with me—first I say, 'No, no, it's impossible, completely and utterly impossible,' then I go ahead and do it."

Ishmael humphed, barely mollified.

"One thing I know people will say to me is, 'Are you suggesting we go back to being hunter-gatherers?'"

"That of course is an inane idea," Ishmael said. "The Leaver life-style isn't about hunting and gathering, it's about letting the rest of the community live—and agriculturalists can do that as well as hunter-gatherers." He paused and shook his head. "What I've been at pains to give you is a new paradigm of human history. The Leaver life is not an antiquated thing that is 'back there' somewhere. Your task is not to reach back but to reach forward."

"But to what? We can't just walk away from our civilization the way the Hohokam did."

"That's certainly true. The Hohokam had another way of life waiting for them, but you must be inventive—if it's worthwhile to you. If you care to survive." He gave me a dull stare. "You're an inventive people, aren't you? You pride yourselves on that, don't you?"

"Yes."

"Then invent." ·

10

"I have neglected one small point," Ishmael said, then gave way to a long, groaning, wheezing sigh, as if he were sorry he'd allowed himself to be reminded of it.

I waited in silence.

"One of my students was an ex-convict. An armed robber, as it happened. Have I told you that?"

I said he hadn't.

"I'm afraid our work together was more useful to me than

to him. Primarily what I learned from him is that, contrary to the impression one receives from prison movies, the prison population is not at all an undifferentiated mass. As in the outside world, there are the rich and the poor, the powerful and the weak. And relatively speaking, the rich and the powerful live very well inside the prison—not as well as they do on the outside, of course, but much, much better than the poor and the weak. In fact, they can have very nearly anything they want, in terms of drugs, food, sex, and service."

I cocked an eyebrow at him.

"You want to know what this has to do with anything," he said with a nod. "It has this to do with anything: The world of the Takers is one vast prison, and except for a handful of Leavers scattered across the world, the entire human race is now inside that prison. During the last century every remaining Leaver people in North America was given a choice: to be exterminated or to accept imprisonment. Many chose imprisonment, but not many were actually capable of adjusting to prison life."

"Yes, that seems to be the case."

Ishmael fixed me with a drooping, moist eye. "Naturally a well-run prison must have a prison industry. I'm sure you see why."

"Well . . . it helps to keep the inmates busy, I suppose. Takes their minds off the boredom and futility of their lives."

"Yes. Can you name yours?"

"Our prison industry? Not offhand. I suppose it's obvious."

"Quite obvious, I would say."

I gave it some thought. "Consuming the world."

Ishmael nodded. "Got it on the first try."

11

"There is one significant difference between the inmates of your criminal prisons and the inmates of your cultural prison: The former understand that the distribution of wealth and power inside the prison has nothing to do with justice."

I blinked at him for a while, then asked him to explain.

"In your cultural prison, which inmates wield the power?"

"Ah," I said. "The male inmates. Especially the white male inmates."

"Yes, that's right. But you understand that these white male inmates are indeed inmates and not warders. For all their power and privilege—for all that they lord it over everyone else in the prison—not one of them has a key that will unlock the gate."

"Yes, that's true. Donald Trump can do a lot of things I can't, but he can no more get out of the prison than I can. But what does this have to do with justice?"

"Justice demands that people other than white males have power in the prison."

"Yes, I see. But what are you saying? That this isn't true?"

"True? Of course it's true that males—and, as you say, especially white males—have called the shots inside the prison for thousands of years, perhaps even from the beginning. Of course it's true that this is unjust. And of course it's true that power and wealth within the prison should be equitably redistributed. But it should be noted that what is crucial to your survival as a race is not the redistribution of power and wealth within the prison but rather the destruction of the prison itself."

"Yes, I see that. But I'm not sure many other people would."

"No?"

"No. Among the politically active, the redistribution of wealth and power is . . . I don't know what to call it that would be strong enough. An idea whose time has come. The Holy Grail."

"Nonetheless, breaking out of the Taker prison is a common cause to which all humanity can subscribe."

I shook my head. "I'm afraid it's a cause to which almost none of humanity will subscribe. White or colored, male or female, what the people of this culture want is to have as much wealth and power in the Taker prison as they can get. They don't give a damn that it's a prison and they don't give a damn that it's destroying the world."

Ishmael shrugged. "As always, you're a pessimist. Perhaps you're right. I hope you're wrong."

"I hope so too, believe me."

12

Even though we'd only been talking an hour or so, Ishmael seemed limp with exhaustion. I made tentative noises about leaving, but he evidently had something more on his mind.

At last he looked up and said: "You understand that I'm finished with you."

I think it would have felt about the same if he'd plunged a knife into my stomach.

He closed his eyes for a moment. "Pardon me. I'm tired and not expressing myself well. I didn't mean that the way it came out."

I couldn't answer him, but I managed a nod.

"I mean only that I've finished what I set out to do. As a teacher, I have nothing more to give you. Even so, I would be pleased to count you as a friend."

Again, I couldn't manage more than a nod.

Ishmael shrugged and looked around bleary-eyed, as if he'd momentarily forgotten where he was. Then he reared back and exploded in a magnificently juicy sneeze.

"Look," I said, getting up, "I'll be back tomorrow."

He gave me a long, dark stare; he was wondering what the devil more I expected of him but was too weary to ask. He sent me on my way with a grunt and a valedictory nod.

THIRTEEN

1

     That night, before falling asleep in my motel bed, I finalized my plan. It was a bad plan and I knew it, but I couldn't think of anything better. Whether he liked it or not (and I knew he wouldn't), I had to rescue Ishmael from that goddamned carnival.

It was a bad plan in another sense, in that it depended entirely on me and my meager resources. I had only one hole-card, and if I had to turn it, I figured it would probably be a deuce.

At nine the next morning I was in a small town about halfway home, driving around in hopes of finding someplace to have breakfast, when a "too hot" warning lit up on my dashboard, forcing me to pull over. I popped the hood and checked the oil: oil okay. Checked the water reservoir: dry. No problem—a canny traveler, I carry extra water. I topped off the reservoir, got going again, and two minutes later watched the warning light blink back on. I made it to a filling station where the sign said "Mechanic on Duty" but where no mechanic was on duty. Even so, the guy who *was* on duty knew thirty times as much as I do about cars and was willing to poke around a little.

"The radiator fan isn't working," he told me after about fifteen seconds. He showed it to me and explained that ordinarily it only comes on when start-and-stop city driving makes the engine overheat.

"Could it be a blown fuse?"

"Could be," he said. But he ruled that out by trying a new one, which did no better than the old one. He said, "Hold on," and fetched a pen-type probe, which he used to test the plug that connected the fan to the electrical system. "You got fire to the fan," he told me, "so it looks like it's the fan itself that's shot."

"Where can I get a new one?"

"Here in town, nowhere," he told me. "Not on a Saturday."

I asked him if I could get home with it as it was.

"I think so," he said, "if you don't have to do a lot of city driving to get there. Or if you stop and let it cool down whenever it starts to overheat."

I made it back and got the car into a dealership service garage well before noon and left it there, even though they assured me that nothing at all would happen to it before Monday morning. I had only one errand to run, and that was to visit one of those dear little money machines, where I proceeded to plunder all my cash resources—checking, savings, credit cards. When I walked into my apartment, I was carrying twenty-four hundred dollars—and was otherwise a pauper.

I didn't intend to think about the problems ahead, because they were just too tough. How do you get a half-ton gorilla out of a cage that he doesn't care to vacate? How do you get a half-ton gorilla into the back seat of a car that he doesn't care to ride in? Would a car with a half-ton gorilla in the back seat even function?

As this indicates, I'm a one-step-at-a-time kind of guy. An improvisor. Somehow or another, I would get Ishmael stashed in the back seat of my car, then I'd figure out what to do next. Presumably I'd bring him back to my apartment—and then again figure out what to do next. In my experience, you never really know how you're going to handle a problem until you actually have it.

2

They called at nine on Monday morning to tell me what was what with the car. The fan had gone out because it had been overtaxed; it had been overtaxed because the whole damn cooling system was shot. A lot of work was needed, about six hundred dollars' worth. I groaned and told them to carry on. They said it'd probably be ready around two o'clock, they'd call. I said, skip the call, I'd pick the car up when I could; the fact is, I'd already abandoned the car. I couldn't afford the repairs, and the damn thing probably wouldn't be up to carrying Ishmael anyway.

I rented a van.

You will doubtless wonder why in hell I didn't do that in the first place. The answer is, I just didn't think of it. I'm limited, okay? I get used to doing things in a certain way, and that doesn't include taking trips in rented vans.

Two hours later I pulled up at the carnival lot and said, "Damn."

The carnival had moved on.

Something—maybe a premonition—prompted me to get out and poke around. The lot seemed much too small to have held nineteen rides, twenty-four games, and a side-show. I wondered if I could find the site of Ishmael's cage without any landmarks to guide me. My feet remembered enough to get me to the vicinity, and my eyes did the rest, for there *was* a visible trace: the blankets I'd bought for him had been left behind, had been dumped in a messy pile along with other things I recognized: a few of his books, a pad of drawing paper, still showing the maps and diagrams he'd made to illustrate the stories of Cain and Abel, Leavers and Takers, and the poster from his office, now rolled up and secured by a rubber band.

I was stirring it up and sorting it out in a bewildered way when my aged bribee turned up. He grinned and held up a big black plastic bag to show me what he was doing there: clearing away some of the hundreds of pounds of trash that had been left behind. Then, when he saw the pile of stuff at my feet, he looked up at me and said, "It was the pneumonia."

"What?"

"It was the pneumonia that got him—your friend the ape."

I stood there blinking at him, unable to fathom what he was getting at.

"Vet came Saturday night and shot him full of stuff, but it was too late. Passed off this morning around seven or eight, I guess."

"Are you telling me that he's . . . dead?"

"Dead is what he is, pardner."

And I, the total egotist, had only vaguely registered the fact that he seemed a bit wan.

I looked around the vast gray lot, where here and there

the wind raised clumps of paper trash and sometimes sent them tumbling, and felt one with it—empty, useless, choked with dust, a wasteland.

My ancient pardner waited, plainly interested to see what this friend of apes would do or say next.

"What did they do with him?" I asked.

"Huh?"

"What did they do with the body?"

"Oh. Called the county, I guess. Took him off to where they cremate the roadkills. You know."

"Yeah. Thanks."

"No sweat."

"All right if I take this stuff?"

From the look he gave me I could see I'd presented him with a new high-water mark in human lunacy, but all he said was, "Sure, why not? Just get dumped otherwise."

I left the blankets, of course, but the rest all fit easily under one arm.

3

What was to be done? Stand for a moment with lowered gaze outside the county furnace where they cremate the roadkills? Someone else would have handled it differently, probably better, revealing a greater heart, a finer sensibility. Myself, I drove home.

Drove home, turned in the van, picked up my car, and went back to the apartment. It was empty in a new way, with a new degree of emptiness.

There was a telephone there on an end table, connecting me to a whole world of life and activity, but who could I call?

Oddly enough, I thought of someone, looked up a number, and dialed it. After three rings, a low, firm voice answered:

"Mrs. Sokolow's residence."

"Is this Mr. Partridge?"

"Yes, this is Mr. Partridge."

I said, "This is the guy who visited you a couple weeks ago, trying to locate Rachel Sokolow."

Partridge waited.

I said, "Ishmael is dead."

After a pause: "I'm very sorry to hear it."

"We could have saved him."

Partridge thought about that for a while. "Are you sure he would have let us?"

I wasn't sure, and said so.

4

It wasn't till I got Ishmael's poster to the framing shop that I discovered there were messages on both sides. I had it framed so that both can be seen. The message on one side is the one Ishmael displayed on the wall of his den:

WITH MAN GONE,
WILL THERE
BE HOPE
FOR GORILLA?

The message on the other side reads:

WITH GORILLA GONE,
WILL THERE
BE HOPE
FOR MAN?

A Note to the Reader

Ishmael has always been much more than a book to me. It's my hope that it will be much more than a book to many of those who read it. If you are one of this number, I hope you'll do me the favor of getting in touch.

Therefore, I hereby provide an address I can maintain indefinitely for the small cost of renting a post office box: Box 163686, Austin, TX 78716-3686.

Who knows? Perhaps if there are enough of us, we can get something started here.

That's what it's all about, isn't it?

ABOUT THE AUTHOR

DANIEL QUINN was born in Omaha, Nebraska, in 1935 and studied at St. Louis University, the University of Vienna in Austria, and Loyola University of Chicago. In 1975 he abandoned a long career in publishing in Chicago to become a free-lance writer.

The first version of the book that ultimately became of *Ishmael*, his award-winning novel, was written in 1977 and was followed by seven more complete and distinct versions. "I was ready to admit defeat when Ted Turner announced his plans for the Turner Tomorrow Fellowship. I felt that, if I read him right, he was looking for exactly the sort of book I was struggling to write, and this encouraged me to give it one more try. I'm certainly glad I did."

Daniel Quinn lives with his wife, Rennie, in Austin, Texas, where he is at work on another novel.